SWEET, SWEET JAYNE

First Edition: October 2019

Cover by The Cover Collection. Interior designed by Nuno Moreira, NM DESIGN

Edited by Carl McCarthy

Copyedited by Ryan Quinn

Proofread by Allister Thompson

Published by Cnoc Máirtín Press of Pelham, New Hampshire

cnocmairtinpress.com

instagram.com/trmonaghanauthor

ISBN 978-1-7336391-0-1 Hardcover

ISBN 978-1-7336391-1-8 Paperback

ISBN 978-1-7336391-2-5 eBook

Library of Congress Control Number: 2019915032

FOR MY MOTHER AND FATHER

SWEET,

a novel

SWEET

T.R. MONAGHAN

JAYNE

To dare is to lose one's footing momentarily. Not to dare is to lose oneself.

—Søren Aabye Kierkegaard

CHAPTER ONE

Jayne Regina-Marie Ranney was too mature to lose herself in the mythical land of Pufnstufs, Whilhelmina Whitchiepoo, and The Good Trees. Although if she let her imagination run, she was sure to find their real-world counterparts in the city. No, from a young age, she dealt realistically with whatever came down the pike.

At the moment, it was letting out a short, high-pitched scream as Rick Trevino tugged her head back by the hair. The moment was quick and her eyes watered. She threw her hand up to soothe the spot on her head as she stood in the entrance to the school cafeteria.

"Why?" Jayne asked.

He studied her reaction, her face, as if feeding off the shock and the pain. He and his cousin Elliot were a tag team of sorts, and she was far from their only victim. They targeted the quiet kids, girls and boys. The kids who didn't fit in. Ones who were little threat to the two who, in early spring, lifted Jayne by her arms so her feet dangled and walked her into the boys' restroom. There were boys at the urinals and three older kids by the window smoking cigarettes. They had all erupted into laughter as she struggled to get free, kicking her legs, shutting her eyes tight as her face reddened.

The memory only added to the anger rising in Jayne. She was sorry she stowed her math and science books in her locker. They would have been a great weapon to swing at Rick, below the belt. Wipe the satisfied look from his face as he walked around her, farther into the lunchroom. She rubbed the back of her head. If she had learned anything in her fifteen years, it was to stay out of the way, don't be a burden, and if someone hurts you, fight back or suck up the pain.

It would not come as a surprise to hear Rick and Elliot had stepped up their game in the past year, torturing small animals or lighting fires on a whim. Thankfully, they had a lot of distractions and had not focused their sole attention or madness on her. She did her best, she thought, to melt into the background. She was small, with pale skin and long, brown hair parted down the center of her head. Her father had told her she was beautiful. He said her blue eyes shined when she smiled. That when she laughed, the sound blew off his worries like wind on the seeds of a dandelion. But he was biased, and she had not heard him speak those words in a very long time. Very few people had made her laugh since.

She headed for the lunch line and dug change out of her pocket for a square of the pizza and tater tots on offer for lunch. The green beans would remain in their designated square on the tray, uneaten. You couldn't say no to the vegetable, so it would be emptied into the trash at the end of the period.

Jayne set her food onto the long table as she sat on the bench seat across from Émile Savard, a friend she had grown closer to in woodshop this last semester. With everything she did at home, she had been determined not to waste two and a half hours a week in home economics. Even if shop was dominated by the boys.

Émile wore his Buddy Holly eyeglasses with pride, no matter how much ribbing he received. He never invited trouble, but he was of the right height and size to defend himself in either case. She thought of him as a bear, big and lovable until seriously poked. Then step back or lose a limb.

He opened his small carton of milk and drank, needing help swallowing the crustless square of pizza he managed to finish in four bites. He wore a *Keep on Truckin'* T-shirt. Its proliferation on merchandise was a trend the artist Robert Crumb was said to despise.

"Hi," Jayne said. She tapped her palm on her head to ease the sting. "What's up?"

"Ricky Trevino. Pulled out some hair."

Émile finished his milk and crushed the carton in his hand. "I'm going to kill him."

"Don't. You might beat Ricky down, but he and that psycho Elliot will come back at you twice as hard. They'll push you in front of a bus or plunk a lawn dart in your chest. Besides, they haven't messed with me in months. I can handle a trip in the hall, a few hairs out of my head."

"Well, I'll hurt him if you want. Just say the word."

She lifted the cold pizza up in her hand. "I'll let you know."

"They deserve more than a beatdown." He pulled at the collar of his T-shirt. "You want to do something after school?"

"Can't today. I'm meeting my brother."

"He's out?"

"Yup. Don't know where he's been crashing, though."

Émile maneuvered out from the bench seat and grabbed up his tray. "I gotta jet. See you tomorrow?"

"You know it."

≈

Jayne's tether to her family was not strong.

Terence Ranney, her father, died when she was nine. He drove south in the winters, loaded up with tools in his pickup for odd jobs. His last trip down was in September of '65. Terry drove farther south than he had ever done in the past to assist in cleanup efforts in Louisiana after Hurricane

Betsy. He made use of his chainsaw to section downed branches on private property. The homeowner, inexperienced in the use of his own, cut the base of a leaning tree. It kicked out and threw Terry ten feet in the air to be impaled on a limb that was torn jagged to a fine point by the storm.

A friend of the Ranney family stepped in to bring her father's body back to be buried. As she stood next to Margaret and Michael in the church pew and tears streamed down her face, she remembered the only comfort being a large, warm hand on her shoulder. A man standing in the pew behind her rested his hand there throughout the service and took up the task again at the cemetery.

Out of school for the day, Jayne hurried down Thorndike Street to the South Common, hoping Michael would be there as promised. She would not be surprised if he let her down, but her anger would return. It was one of the few emotions she relished lately. An emotion she could sink her teeth into.

She saw him in the distance, and as she got closer, he appeared to finish business with a guy who turned heel and headed up the hill in the direction of the courthouse. Michael looked good. His hair had grown a few inches, and he brushed it back twice from his eyes before she reached him. She hoped he had found a place to live, although she would never ask. She hoped he wasn't back to showering at the Y across the way, stowing his clothes and belongings in a locker.

"Sis. How've you been?" He put his hands in the front pockets of his jeans and swayed on his feet.

The Ranneys were not huggers. Jayne's last hugs were when she was put to bed by their father.

"You and Mom getting along okay?" he asked.

"You know Margaret. I keep to myself, she's happy."

He reached behind the park bench and pulled over his bicycle. "Happy birthday, sis."

"My birthday's not for another three weeks."

He shrugged. "I got the season right, though, right?"

"You're giving me your old bike?"

He pulled it closer to her side. "I taped the handles for you. See? Lowered the seat all the way. Go ahead, hop up."

She grabbed the handlebar, tilted the bicycle, and swung her leg over the horizontal bar, clearing it by only a quarter inch. A step on a pedal and she was on the seat, the very tips of her toes grazing the pavement as the bicycle listed.

Michael reached out and grabbed under the back of the seat to steady it. "You start pedaling, it will straighten right out."

Jayne got off but kept hold of the handlebar. "Thanks."

He smiled. "You remember how to get ahold of me?"

"I remember." Jayne eased the bicycle forward and started back on the path to the road.

"All right, then," he said. He sat down on the bench and stretched out his legs, crossing them at the ankles. He slipped his hands back in his front pockets.

Jayne reached the road and used the drop of the sidewalk edge to climb back up on the bicycle. She turned back to see Michael, but he was gone. Disappeared, as if he were never there in the first place.

CHAPTER TWO

Michael walked across a bridge, over steel grating that spanned its length high above the Merrimack River. Through the soles of his shoes, he felt the hum of vibration from the mass of water running below. He glimpsed shadows of its power in the darkness after the week of heavy rain.

Upriver, the current was fast and strong as it crested the wooden flashboards of Pawtucket Falls. In its southward course, the Merrimack River sliced down a side of the city and fed a canal system. During the industrial era, those tributaries were the heart valves, pumping lifeblood downtown. But by 1960, manufacturing had slowed to a crawl, unemployment numbers climbed, and the city and its infrastructure sank into decay. Its people, as a consequence, grew strong and more resilient in the face of adversity.

Michael stepped off the curb in the direction of the George Chadwick Memorial School. In the distance, the white tail of a deer caught his eye. Michael looked on as the large animal turned its upper body to glance back at him and made its way through a patch of trees. Closing in on 3:00 a.m., little else moved. A rustling of tree branches. A few pieces of trash skittering across the road on the wind.

Michael's jeans hung low on his hips, weighed down by bolt cutters, a wrench, screwdriver, and a Zippo. He carried his wallet in a back pocket, secured by a length of chain to a belt loop. A flashlight was tucked in an inside pocket of his jacket. He flipped up his collar and pushed his hair

7

out of his eyes. He tugged on the edges of his wool knit cap to cover and warm the tops of his ears.

The Chadwick School stood ahead, diminished from its former grandeur after closing the previous spring. The school budget was strained after a project to reinforce the foundation on its river side and one to update the heating system. The cumulative debt and additional repairs needed for the building to pass inspection both factored in its closure.

Michael stopped at the corner of the building and turned his head in all directions. He trudged down the alley, following the rough brick with his fingertips. He reached the farthest of the wide, sunken window wells, removed his cap, and held it against the pane of glass. He broke through with his wrench and cleared around the frame in a fast and efficient manner. He took two swats of his cap against his thigh to dislodge any glass shards and tucked it away. He donned a pair of gloves and entered, his leather jacket and blue jeans working as protection against protruding glass as he dropped into the boiler room.

He had arrived alone to harvest copper, even though the job warranted another two hands. Michael needed every dollar the metal could generate. He began the task in earnest and moved within the cramped recesses of the ceilings and walls. Copper often traveled with electrical lines, so earlier in the week he had confirmed there was no live power to the building. He planned to gather as much scrap material as he could pull before daylight. He would return the next night with a borrowed van to load and cart away his haul. Overgrown brush running alongside the building would likely hide the broken window for twenty-four hours. He would remember to pack the well with downed leaves before leaving.

Moonlight and streetlight streamed through upper windows, but deep darkness permeated the inner sections of the building. Michael illuminated a path with his flashlight to avoid a stumble over forgotten furniture and debris. Within the hour, he made his way over an air duct in the ceiling of the kitchen to get at the pipes. He held his flashlight ahead of him and pulled his body forward on the weight of his forearms. He gasped in pain, halting from a catch on the soft skin above his hipbone. He lifted himself so his shoulders brushed the pipes above and glanced down the long length of his body. Backing his way out would cause more damage. He snaked one of his hands down to test the hold of a protruding metal bolt. He kicked a leg out farther to lift his midsection.

On the second try to free himself, and in the struggle, the duct below him gave way. On impact with the concrete floor, his breath was expelled with force. He writhed in pain, gulping in air three, four times before successfully inflating his lungs. He cursed and moaned on a halted exhale as he turned onto his side. He sat up and stared at his lap, where a bloodstain bloomed a deep red from above his hip. Michael registered the pain as an awakening pulse before the sensation soon moved on to a steady rhythm of hurt. His right side from hip to knee had taken the brunt of the impact. He stood and leaned his weight on a cabinet counter. He looked to the ceiling and shook his head. Lately, there had not been one job that had gone off as planned.

He limped around the kitchen, searching for material to fashion a compress. He did not want to have to resort to removing his undershirt to prevent the stream of blood running down his leg from leaving a trail in its wake. In a small office at the back of the room, he located an apron on the floor of a supply cabinet. He folded the material and stuffed one half of it down the waist of his jeans. Michael held his hand over the makeshift bandage. He had suffered far worse injuries than the current flesh wound on his hip. Attempting to take the fall in stride, he decided on one last task before cutting the job short.

Michael walked a long hallway toward the gymnasium to check for any exposed copper in the shower rooms. As he reached the locker room door, he heard what sounded like voices. He approached the entrance to the gym, limping and lumbering, and peeked around the wide doorframe. Two men stood near center court in scant light that filtered through a narrow row of high windows.

Michael maneuvered closer by sliding behind a wall of collapsed bleachers. He peered out from a two-inch gap in flat slats of wood. He recognized Sergeant Ray Hamel on hearing the brash tone of his voice echoing off the walls. The sergeant also gestured in a familiar manner with his hands as he spoke. They'd had a few run-ins in the past, beginning with Officer Hamel pulling Michael out of his grade-school class for questioning about a stolen bicycle. Michael remembered that first encounter clearly. He had professed innocence and managed to exchange the bike hours later for a couple of prized baseball cards.

Michael wiped dirt and grease from his brow and pulled his hand through his hair as he moved it from in front of his eyes. He braced an arm on the wood and rested his forehead forward.

Ray Hamel, in street clothes, stood with his profile to Michael. The sergeant quieted. His tongue moved over his upper teeth. The stranger was expressionless. He wore a crisp navy suit tailored to a lean frame. His polished black shoes had a shine even in the meager light. To Michael, the other man's appearance suggested a rank far above sergeant, and he would lay odds the man was from a branch of government or law enforcement other than the LPD.

Sergeant Hamel smacked his gums. "Enough with the silent treatment and your failure to grasp what I'm offering. I called this get-together, but what goddamn time is this?"

"I was in town. Late. I only found your note under my door when I got back. I don't like you coming by my hotel, by the way. You reach me by phone from now on, and if I can't talk, I'll call you back." The man crossed his arms over his chest and widened his stance. "Want to tell me why we're here?"

"Why'd they pull you in to Boston?"

The man shrugged in response.

Hamel slid his hands into his front pockets and swayed on his feet. "I know you're in other towns. This ain't the only spot. Shaking down dealers and skimming from SHARE. The trough's got to be deep. And a capable man like you, you're pulling a healthy sum by my calculation. How long before someone catches on? Even in your position, how've you been getting away with your shenanigans?"

"Nixon sent me north. And to me, doing a little walking around with sticky fingers proves how dire the problem is on both sides. Lot of balls in the air before this all goes federal, so I've got wiggle room."

"How about you slide me a piece of pie while you suss it all out?"

The man shook his head in resignation and lowered his arms to his sides. "What the hell are you doing up in my things, anyways?"

"That's my office," Hamel said with a hint of a smile at play on his lips.

"While out on a medical, you stop and riffle through my locked briefcase. My personal belongings."

"Again, my office." Hamel picked at an incisor with his thumbnail.

"Give me a couple days."

Sergeant Hamel's expression became deadpan. "You've got until Friday. I'm an asset and I'll earn my take."

"Fine. Fine. Where'd you park?"

"Nowhere. I live two streets over."

As the weight of the verbal exchange settled on Michael Ranney's mind, he breathed at a slow, calm, and steady rate. He prayed to remain undetected. The two men turned and made their way to the exit at the far wall, and Michael's shoulders slumped in relief.

Halfway to the door, the man in the suit stepped flush to Ray Hamel's back. He hooked his right arm around the shorter man's neck.

Sergeant Hamel expelled a quick breath of surprise. He struggled to break free, pushing back with his body and pulling on the stiff arm at his neck. He attempted to swing his weight to the side but failed. The attacker pulled him in tight, Ray's back to the tall man's chest. The suit grasped his own fist and tightened the hold as if channeling Johnny Weaver. Ray's carotid arteries and jugular veins had certainly ceased the flow of blood to the brain. The man eased Hamel to the floor and kept a steady hold, long after Hamel's window to tap out slammed shut.

Michael's whole body tensed, and he was still, like a rabbit in a field witnessing a sibling snatched up by a red-tailed hawk. He watched the cold, calm actions of the killer with awe.

The man set Hamel on his back and straddled the prone body without seeming to put weight on Hamel's chest. The suit placed two fingers on pulse points at Hamel's neck and wrist. Then he stood and straightened the back of his suit jacket. He ran his thumbs down the inside of his lapels and left the gym.

Michael let out the breath he had been holding. His fear caused a small tremor in his hands. But the pain at his hip fell silent as a spike of adrenaline pumped through his veins. The gym door swung wide and banged like a shot as it hit the wall. The killer dropped a concrete block to keep it ajar. He exited and returned to the darkness. He was gone only a few minutes before reverse and brake lights lit the area within the doorway.

Michael crouched low.

The man entered with a large cloth tarp and rolled Hamel within the material. His efforts facilitated an easy drag of the body out the door. A series of bangs followed, and panting from exertion. The stranger reached inside the door and retrieved the concrete block, and after a metallic thud the gym fell silent.

Michael moved out from the bleachers and, with his back on the wall, slid his butt to the floor. He tilted his head back and calmed his nerves.

He could not have picked a worse time and a worse place. He stood with effort and made his way to the same exit. He eased the unsecured door open and slipped into the early morning, abandoning any thought of returning.

There would be thirteen homicides in the city by end of year. Only twelve were officially recorded.

CHAPTER THREE

Michael craned his neck around the back corner of the Skillet Bar.

Out at the street, Tao Mann, the establishment's bartender, looked both ways and stepped into the road. Tao lifted his arm to wave at the driver of a plumbing truck as he quickened his step and crossed Market Street. He made his way down the alley toward the back entrance. He pulled keys from his coat pocket and kicked up loose gravel with his boots. He glanced over at an overflowing dumpster and swore. The coldness of the crisp morning air kept any strong odors at bay. Tao rounded the corner and pulled up short. He greeted Michael with a curt nod.

Michael kept a shoulder against the brick wall and inhaled the tail end of a joint. He dropped the spent roach to the ground and leaned forward. He looked once again down the length of the dirt alley.

"What brings you out of the woodwork this time of day?" Tao asked.

Michael unbuttoned and pulled open his jacket. He revealed the soiled apron jammed down his side and the dark bloodstain that now reached mid-thigh. His walk to the bar from across the river was not the wisest of his decisions.

Tao raised an eyebrow as he readied a key and opened the back door.

Michael hesitated a moment to peer back at the street. He turned, lifted off the wall, and followed Tao inside. A fog had settled on Michael's brain, caused by a lack of sleep and the shock of earlier events. The marijuana, after years of daily exposure, was of little consequence.

Tao walked the hall and approached the end of the bar. He

15

leaned over the surface and pulled up a heavy rotary phone with a long, tangled cord. Michael stood a few feet away as Tao dialed and gave Michael his back.

"Need you down here. Bring your kit," Tao said into the line.

Michael felt unsteady on his feet and reached out to lean on the bar for support.

"No. Not for me—for Michael Ranney," Tao said. He glanced back and frowned. "Nope. They still have a game going on upstairs. You're going to have to make do with the bar." Tao replaced the receiver in its cradle and reached over to turn up the thermostat on the wall. The boiler in the basement kicked on with a bang, and he motioned to one of the stools. "Hang tight. Jimmy's on his way. You want to make the call?"

Michael shook his head.

Tao stepped back toward the office by the back door. "I'll go give Galen a shout then."

Michael leaned more of his upper-body weight on the bar top and sat on the very edge of a stool.

Tao soon returned from the office. He set his long hair back in an elastic tie and went about cleaning and stocking the bar without offering up conversation.

Michael's chin sank to his chest, and his mind shut down. In what felt like a moment, he came alert at the back door swinging shut.

Jimmy "Tens" arrived, and after a few short words with Tao, he set up on one of the low tables across the floor. He pulled out supplies from a leather doctor's bag and filled a metal bowl with water from the sink behind the bar. He crossed the floor to the men's room, holding a small towel from his kit. He propped open the door with a trash can and leaned over the sink. He held a small brush that he grasped tight and scrubbed both his hands and his forearms. He turned off the faucet with the edge of the towel and stepped back into the room.

Michael stood from the stool. A stab of pain radiated down his leg, along with a stiffness that had moved into his bruised muscles while he was stationary. He limped over with a grimace as Jimmy sat and snapped on a pair of medical gloves with a flourish. Michael removed his coat and the heavy burglary gear from his pockets. He pushed his jeans and underwear to his thighs to allow Jimmy access to the wound. Michael turned his head and looked over his shoulder at Tao.

The bartender looked on from across the room with an expression of disdain. "Nice ass, Michael. But how about giving the man there your attention?"

Michael looked at Jimmy's hands on his hip. "I appreciate this."

Jimmy sat straight and poured a small amount of salt into the bowl of warm water. "This ain't no knife. What jumped out and bit ya?"

"Metal bolt."

"Lay back on the table before you fall," Jimmy said.

Michael shuffled around and maneuvered onto the Formica-topped table. He was glad to be off his feet as his legs dangled over the edge. And he was fortunate the table had an iron base and held his weight. He lasted only a moment on his elbows before lowering himself flat. He took a deep, cleansing breath and slowed the erratic beat of his heart.

Jimmy cleaned the outer area of the wound with a small square cloth. He poured water over Michael's hip, washing blood and detritus onto the table and floor.

In response, Michael pulled in air through his clenched teeth. He relaxed his limbs the best he was able and resisted the urge to bolt from the table.

Jimmy grabbed a pair of long tweezers from the row of instruments laid out on the bench. He probed the open wound and pulled away dirt and fibers left by the cloth apron. "You sure you want me stitching this? It's a jagged tear. I do this, I'll leave my mark."

"Do it. I don't care about no scar."

Jimmy lifted his head and called over to the bar. "You got any spare clothes here? He can free-ball it, but he's going to need some walking-around threads."

Tao shook his head. "Nope."

Jimmy pulled a needle out from a sealed package and threaded a suture. He leaned back over the wound. "He ain't ever going to warm up to you, is he?"

Michael stared at a repeating pattern on the ceiling. "I don't know what his deal is."

"Really? You don't recall making a blatant pass at him at the Commodore. In front of a club full of people, no less. Knowing Tao doesn't swing that way. You're lucky he didn't punch your teeth through the back of your head. It reminded me of the fights you got into back in school. When you went that one step too far to test kids. The ones that wouldn't give you the time of day. And to prove what?"

"You're wrong."

"So you thought you'd get lucky? With Tao? You thought—he's not ignoring me, only denying his urges. Never thought of you as that stupid."

"A bit of dry humping, and he gets all bent out of shape."

Jimmy shook his head. "Lie back so I can get at this thing. You got a ride? How far you going from here?"

"Clare Street," Michael said.

"I'll swing you by if you want. So, you're not walking Broadway, buck naked. You can change before we hit St. Joe's for a tetanus shot."

Michael, with a half-lidded, curious look on his face, peered down his torso at Jimmy.

"You're not getting out of it. So don't waste your breath," Jimmy said and turned his head. "Tao, throw me one of those bar towels and bring over some anesthetic."

Tao arrived with a bottle and the addition of a rocks glass. He poured a drink, pulled the towel off his shoulder, and lobbed it over Michael's privates.

Jimmy nodded once and met his patient's eyes as Michael lifted back onto his elbows. "That thing so much as twitches, you're doing the needlepointing."

Michael breathed in deep with Jimmy's first stitch. He grabbed the glass from Tao and downed the harsh whiskey. He rested his head back on the firm surface, and the liquor burned the back of his throat, bringing heat to his gut. As he hummed a strained chorus of "Spill the Wine," Jimmy sealed the wound and the sharp pains ceased. Michael felt a cool salve applied to his skin.

Jimmy ripped open a paper packet and taped on a large gauze bandage. His medical skills were rarely needed at the bar because violence seldom broke out at the Skillet. The last fight he could remember was an anomaly. That night, a pint glass was the weapon. The altercation had Galen "the Greek" Stathakis resort to serving beer in pull-tab cans. For two days, that is. Jimmy was still amazed the guy on the receiving end survived. He had stemmed the flow of blood from the man's neck. The bar quieted eerily until the arrival of an ambulance. The brawl brought the bar up for review by the city, and a hastened closing time was imminent. Until the Greek pulled in favors from two city officials on the board.

Galen, the man himself, arrived through the back door. He threw his coat in his office from the hallway and walked over to the surgical table. The big man hovered over Jimmy's shoulder with his arms folded across his chest. They rested on his ample belly.

Jimmy peeled off his gloves and released a pent-up sneeze into the crook of his elbow. "Hey, Galen."

Galen ignored the greeting. "Is that a gunshot wound, Michael?"

"No," Michael said.

"So, why you splayed out here? What's wrong with a hospital?"

"I'm short on green. I couldn't get the bleeding to stop, or I would've patched it up myself—I'll clean all this up."

Galen gestured with his head to Tao and Jimmy to go back to his office as Michael scooted carefully off the table.

Michael cut his underwear from his legs with scissors he grabbed from the table. He eased up his jeans, zipping the ruined pants only halfway to avoid covering the dressing. He swept his underwear, along with the apron and pieces of bloodied gauze, into the metal bowl. He sat gingerly on the very edge of the booth seat. "I have a meeting in a couple days," he said, pulling his fingers through his hair to get the sweat-dampened strands out of his face.

Galen looked down on Michael with a glimmer of amusement in his eyes. "On the recent volatile nature of the Dow?"

"No. With my PO."

"What does a meet with your parole officer have to do with me? The respect and love I have for your late father does not give you free rein to lay *skatá* on me."

Michael poured himself another belt of whiskey. "I've never kept anything from you, Galen. Even told you about that fuck-up in Chelsea I pried my way out of last year." He downed the drink and pushed the glass over the surface of the table, toward the wall. "Thing is, I stepped in something, and my head's all over the place."

"Any blowback coming my way?" Galen said.

"Don't think so."

"Yes or no—now."

"Potential trouble for me and me alone. But I need a favor."

"Careful what you ask, Michael."

Michael took a moment to gather his thoughts.

Galen prompted him with a lift of the chin. "Talk. But keep in mind—if I feel in any way you're taking advantage of my goodwill, I won't be here for you anymore. No bailing you out. No sending a tow for your car when the engine catches fire on 28. No lawyers, no loans, no stitch-up sessions at eight in the morning. Godson or not, you choose your words carefully."

"That wasn't my car…"

"*Maláka*. Speak."

≈

The house on Clare Street sat separate from its neighbors by mere feet on either side. It had a small, well-tended yard in the rear. The front stairs were built on a granite slab set two inches deeper on the right to bring the steps in line with the foundation.

The interior of the house had painted moldings. There was a wide, built-in hutch in the dining room and a floor of well-worn planks in the hallway. They creaked in a spot toward the kitchen, either by foot or seasonal play.

Michael washed with care in a bathroom on the second floor, making the effort to keep his stitches dry. He entered the bedroom as he rubbed a towel over his hair. He pulled aside the curtain to glance at Jimmy idling in his Plymouth Duster 340 at the curb. Michael threw the towel over a chair and pulled on a pair of slacks. He found a V-neck sweater nestled in the bureau drawers. His ruined jeans and T-shirt lay on the floor. He shed the articles of clothing with purpose, knowing full well his host would have a conniption over his careless manner and the sight of dried bloodstains.

Michael finished getting ready. He pulled on his coat and knit cap and remembered to tuck a fresh pack of cigarettes in his pocket. He had been copping from the carton on the bedside table for the past few days. He made his way to the kitchen and paused to scratch the resident tabby cat between the ears. Michael rummaged in the refrigerator for sustenance. He came away with a heel of a loaf of bread from a carved wooden box near the phone. He took little care in scarfing down the hard, dry crust on his way to the front door. He coughed up a few crumbs lodged in his throat before entering the car. He made himself as comfortable as possible in the passenger seat, favoring his tender hip and the massive bruised area on his leg.

Jimmy's attention was on Michael's ankles. "Dude, you expecting a flood?"

"The pants aren't mine." Michael ran his hands down the dark red corduroy in a futile attempt to stretch the material.

"No kidding." Jimmy put the car in gear.

Michael turned his head back to the house as they pulled away from the curb. "I may have overstayed my welcome."

"Man, stealing his clothes is not going to help your cause."

Michael made use of the headrest and closed his eyes for the trip to the clinic. The action worked to signal his reluctance to talk. He used the same tactic in the waiting room for the forty-five minutes they sat.

Jimmy twiddled his thumbs for the duration.

"Mr. Ranney?" a nurse said.

Michael stood and winced. Every step was slow and deliberate, and still his teeth clenched from the pain.

"Third door on your left," she said.

Jimmy followed and on entering the room stood in the corner until the doctor arrived.

The doctor glanced up from his clipboard. "Says here you scraped up against a piece of metal?"

"Something like that. I was told I could get a tetanus shot."

"May I see?"

Michael turned his head to Jimmy and received a near imperceptible nod. He worked the pants over his hip and held the sweater up, out of the way.

The doctor eased off the bandage and inspected the wound. "That, Mr. Ranney, is no scrape. Did we stitch you?"

Michael shook his head. The immediate area of the wound looked inflamed. But the surrounding skin was Michael's normal pale hue.

"It's good work." The doctor palpitated around the stitches with his fingers.

At his praise, a slow smile spread across Jimmy's face. Michael received his booster, and Jimmy peeled off money at the office window to square the bill.

In the car, as they headed out of the lot, Michael lowered the volume on the 8-track player. "How'd you get so good at this?" he said, gesturing to his hip.

"Was a shadow to a medic, in-country, for the tour and a half I served." Jimmy scratched his chin, pulling his fingers through his beard. "I was support to get men to the Hueys. My guy was armed, but his hands were busy, and minutes were life or death. Within two months, I was hands deep in the blood and gore myself. I'd do anything to help my brothers, man. And help was needed."

"You come home early?"

Jimmy nodded. "Bit of a dustup with our platoon leader, a second lieutenant who got me sent stateside."

"This ought to be good."

Another easy smile appeared on Jimmy's face. "Tied the fucker to a tree during a firefight."

"Jesus," Michael said on an exhale.

"He got winged, and a bullet grazed his scalp, nothing serious. He was breathing. The man was crazy. Sent us into all kinds of shit-storms and didn't take any wisdom. He got me my ticket home."

"You in the stockade at all? Serve time?"

"Nah. All my guys backed me. Swore up and down I was on the other side of the clearing. So, no witnesses other than the lieutenant. They stuck by me all the way. The worst the service could do was drum me out." Jimmy turned on his blinker and took a wide right turn as if he was driving an eighteen-wheeler. "Only regret I have is having to leave them. Can't stop thinking about leaving my friends behind." He turned up the Creedence Clearwater Revival track and raised his voice over the music. "Lieutenant Willard was sent home too. Last I heard he was bunking down in a booby hatch outside of Columbus, Ohio." Jimmy gave Michael a wink in closing the conversation and turned his eyes to the road.

CHAPTER FOUR

January 1972

Michael walked down Shattuck Street. Flurries fell and flakes swirled around him with every gust of wind. He raised his face to the sky and felt the cool, wet snow melting on his skin.

It was after 1:00 a.m. on a Tuesday. The streets would soon descend into quiet after the current short burst of activity. Bar patrons stumbled from entrances near closing time. He listened to the din of conversation as people paired off to their cars and peeled off to walk in the direction of university housing.

Michael felt like an outlier, even though he had lived in the city all his life. He had occasion to visit most of the bars over the years. But they were formative years only a local could appreciate. The college students, the ones gesticulating with voices raised at the late hour, traveled their early twenties on a far different road.

He reached the end of the curb and heard a crunch from car tires crawling up on him from the rear. The police cruiser rumbled on cobblestones covered in a half inch of snow and ice. Not particularly unusual conditions for the time of year.

Michael turned and covered his eyes with the back of his hand. The spotlight on the vehicle illuminated the sidewalk.

Inside, Officer Byrd White shifted his cruiser into park. He buttoned the top of his double-breasted uniform, opened the door, and stepped from the car as he settled his hat over hair cropped close to his head. "That you, Ranney?" he asked.

Michael stood in wonder of his own predicament. The night, a cascade of low notes, was ending as expected. He had failed to find a bed, and not an hour earlier he'd put the last dollars from his pocket on a football card. Michael was periodically flush with cash from dealing marijuana, but he kicked back a good percentage to his supplier, and the balance drained through his fingers like fine grains of sand.

"It's me," he said as he leveled his gaze.

"You know the drill. Hands on the hood and spread your legs." The officer's right hand rested on the butt of his service revolver as he walked to the front of his cruiser. "You have any weapons on you?"

Michael stepped off the sidewalk, leaned, and braced his hands as instructed. He feigned surprise when Officer White widened his stance farther with a kick of a boot. "Knife, back pocket."

The officer patted Michael's pockets. He relieved him of his blade and reached behind his own back at the waist for a pair of handcuffs.

Michael had missed an appointment with his parole officer. For three weeks he avoided the adjunct of the court, and the requisite warrant was now at issue. Michael had already come to terms with the result of his failure to meet the conditions of his parole. He was comfortable knowing he would now escape the elements. In the interim, he kept a persistent level of intoxication, confident his time on the street was finite—a dangerous state given overnight temperatures. Michael's demeanor had been somber throughout the past few weeks, and he refused to reach out and offer sex only for a bed. He preferred more control in his life, even if it led him to his present circumstance.

In the past week, the thermometer had seldom climbed above freezing. Even during daylight hours. Michael shuffled around town, keeping barstools warm. He slept overnight on couches and on apartment floors.

He lasted three nights in his own room at his friend John Donato's house in a quiet section of the city. But the man was on the tail end of kicking an addiction and needed looking after. John "Doe" Donato attended daily sessions of a drug treatment program, but there were long nights to get through after each meet and greet. Michael was unable to enjoy a simple beer in the man's presence.

His last night there, John's nerves and patience appeared to be on a fine edge. An argument escalated into a physical altercation over who could sit in the recliner—who had dibs after Michael vacated it, retrieving an English muffin from the toaster. At the memory, he lifted his fingers to the healing cut on his lip.

Next stop was Trisha Anderson's house. The woman could cook, but she lived off Acton Road in Chelmsford and left him too far out from the action with no car.

In desperation, Michael signed in to the city shelter for the last two nights. The thought of crashing at his mother's O'Brien Terrace apartment was untenable. Tonight, Michael walked alone. And after last night's Celtics loss to Detroit, any means he had in the way of cash was spoken for.

Officer White secured Michael in the rear of the cruiser. A faint scent of urine wafted from the floor. It brought on a wave of nausea Michael hoped to rein in for the short ride to the station. Byrd settled into the driver's seat and cranked the heat. He took a moment to glance in the rearview mirror at Michael before shifting the vehicle into drive.

"How've you been, Byrd?" Michael asked as he leaned forward two inches to keep his hands and the cuffs from digging into his back. Michael held no ill will toward the man, even though the two had tussled in past encounters. Michael would be the first to admit he had provoked the civil servant in every instance.

"Been better. My toes are numb. I forgot to stow my wool socks with my gear. Other than that, no worries."

Michael gazed out the side window. He watched light and shadow play across the downtown neighborhood. There was beauty to the night and early morning. It softened hard edges and hid imperfections and provided harbor for those in need of cover. Provided inspiration for those who needed to work up a plan.

They reached the station, and Byrd assisted Michael from the rear seat. Michael kept his eyes down and walked on the cleared walkway with the officer's steady hand on his upper arm. On the street, a tow truck barreled over packed ice and snow, and above sat stars in a murky sky marred by light pollution and cloud cover.

A sudden blast of heat from a steam radiator in the vestibule caused Michael to hesitate with relief. Byrd pushed on his back in the direction of the wide, tall desk Michael had been steered to in the past.

The desk sergeant pushed his *Herald Traveler* to the side as he stood. "What've you got?"

"Michael Robert Ranney. Warrant for parole violations," Byrd said, stamping his right foot. "Mr. Ranney here was taking a stroll nearby. If you could let us in, Danny, I can offer the gentleman some refreshments and a place to hang his hat."

The sergeant hit a release for the door and gestured with an exaggerated sweep of his arm.

Central booking was reached by a long hallway of gray cement block and a painted concrete floor. Their footsteps echoed until they reached a worn wood bench attached to the wall by steel rods. Byrd turned Michael and unlocked one of his cuffs without comment. He lifted his chin for Michael to sit and fastened his wrist to the bench arm. Byrd went through a swinging door to the guardroom, leaving Michael with an older couple. The two were bundled up, wearing resigned expressions about whatever prompted their untethered visit. Michael gave the curious woman a wave with two fingers of his cuffed hand.

After ten minutes, Michael released a low, sustained groan. He flexed his fingers wide and brought them back in, making fists. Blood beaded from two new cracks on his knuckles. The leather gloves he had sported earlier provided protection, but the pair lay discarded under a stool somewhere.

Michael rested his head back against the wall with a thud. He thought through the conversation that he needed to have on a call to his sister Jayne in the morning. He had not spoken with her in over a month, and the tone on his end would no doubt be strained. His utter failure to set his life in order, to support and shelter her away from their mother, ate at him. He missed Jayne, but the guilt that descended on hearing her voice kept him away.

He had left home at sixteen and returned off and on until he took up residence for the first time at the pleasure of the state. Now he would be back inside to finish a sentence on a previous crime. And if common sense served, "The Man" would most certainly tack on more time.

Officer White gave Michael's foot a swift kick on his return to the room, startling the couple who looked on. "Ranney. You need to piss before we get to it?"

"I'm good," Michael said.

Byrd released the cuff from the bench.

Michael was tired as he stood. Tired enough that the thin, scratchy wool blanket he once curled up with in County would be a comfort. Over the next few days, he would strive to make things easier on himself. He would settle back into the institutional mindset with no fight. That meant going to that place in his head where he appreciated small comforts even more, and accepting that his perception of time as a construct was soon to slow to a regimental crawl.

Byrd led him through the door by the arm and secured his wrist to a chair to the left of a hardwood desk. Byrd shed his heavy coat and adjusted his posture in a straight-backed chair. He filled out a form with a pen from his shirt pocket. "Tell me something, Michael? We both grew up in the same housing project, went to the same schools. Why is it, you think, we chose such different paths?"

"Who knows? Did you always aspire to be such a prick?"

Byrd leaned back, crossed his arms over his chest, and turned his full attention on Michael. "In two hours, I'm off. I'll head home, grab a warm bath. There'll be a plate waiting on the top shelf of the fridge, a few cold beers. Then I'll slide under warm blankets and snuggle up to the finest bare ass in the city." One corner of the man's mouth turned up in a smile. He held his right hand up, palm out, as if to swear an oath. "Not bragging. God's honest truth. Tomorrow, in for another tour of the sights of the city, and in two, three years tops, I'll have enough time in to pick my shifts. You? All I see on your horizon, Michael, is three squares a day and cramped quarters for games of slap and tickle."

Michael shook his head in response. He had the distinct impression Byrd was lying about his domestic bliss. Because no one had it that good. "Thought you'd be shooting for a spot on that new 'Lobster Squad' I read about in the *Sun*."

"Be a nice bump in grade and pay," Byrd replied.

"Who came up with that frig'n name?"

"Next time we'll be sure to search you out for an opinion."

"A squad to catch safe crackers and thieves. Anyone that can't spot you boys sitting on them deserves to get nicked."

Byrd looked at Michael's wrist cuffed to the chair. He turned and leaned forward to complete the form. "The violation states that you failed to check in with your parole officer. And drug paraphernalia and cannabis in an amount sufficient to be classified as 'for distribution' were found in a search of your last known address."

"Not my stash."

"The owner of the property begs to differ."

Michael shrugged.

Byrd turned his head, dropped his chin, and raised his eyebrows. "You currently under the influence of narcotics?"

"No. I had shots of Jack tonight and a couple beers." Michael returned Byrd's earlier smile. "Speaking of which, I'm ready to drain the lizard now."

CHAPTER FIVE

Jayne sat up in bed, swung her feet over the edge, and braced the heels of her hands on the mattress. She had managed only six hours of sleep, and the temptation to slide back under the covers was a strong one. It would be an easy step back into the dream, a dream dissipating in the nether reaches of her mind like fog on a pond at first light.

Instead, she pushed herself to stand, grabbed clothes for school, and tucked the articles under her arm. She gazed in a daze at the floor in the bathroom downstairs. At a series of tan, white, and yellow linoleum squares in a chock-a-block pattern. The cold seeped in from the ground to her bare feet, through the concrete foundation and up under the thin tiles. The shower held promise, though. The apartment she lived in, in the Acre, was notorious for drafts. But there was hot water, and it could run hot all morning long.

Jayne lifted her long, faded nightshirt over her head and eased under the spray. She relaxed her limbs and attempted to free her mind, with little success. Yesterday, Michael had phoned from lockup, and she was worried about him. Worried that a court-appointed lawyer wouldn't help this time. Why would the attorney who defended him on the original beef receive pay from the system for a retread of charges? But Michael's woes were not up for discussion during their call. Jayne needed to run an errand for her brother, and the sooner she handled the chore the better.

After Michael's call, Jayne experienced another tongue-lashing from their mother, Margaret. Questions on why Jayne didn't let her talk to her son and why Jayne didn't find it necessary to fill her in on what was happening. It was not as if their mother had ever offered up help before. Michael was on his own, and he knew it. Jayne found it impossible to argue with Margaret, so she remained silent for most of the yelling, nodding in places to attempt to ease the tension.

In the shower, she shaved her legs and stretched to wash Tame Creme Rinse from her hair. She was grateful she had no new marks that accompanied her mother's verbal assault. Standing at arm's length rarely proved far enough. When Michael lived at home, he was Jayne's defender and the one capable of shutting down their mother's tirades. She had become a handy target in his absence.

She plodded forward, though, a bundle of nerves strung tight and deep in her center mass like a fist. She held hard to a frayed strand of a notion that Michael would emerge out of the rabbit hole. To the notion that he would pull himself together and surprise her one day.

Jayne stepped from the shower and dried herself. She wiped condensation from the mirror and shook Margaret's razor free of water. Her expression in her reflection was stoic as she pulled a wide-tooth comb through her hair. The tines felt good on her scalp, and she eased to sit on the towel draped over the side of the tub. The repetitive motion was a comfort.

She dressed, pulling on underwear, a long-sleeve flannel shirt, and a pair of jeans. She returned upstairs and eased open the door to her mother's room. Jayne placed the razor back in the top drawer of the dresser. Remnants of an ever-present alcoholic haze kept Margaret's figure still and dead to the world.

Jayne headed to the kitchen. She pulled a flathead screwdriver from the back of the utensil drawer. Michael's instruction on the call had been cryptic but obvious. She climbed the stairs and entered his room. She pulled out old blankets stuffed into the bottom of the closet and revealed a large paint can. The label was too worn to read. She lifted the thin wire handle from the side and pulled it toward her as she sat cross-legged on the floor. She used the tool to pry open the lid, revealing Michael's stash of keepsakes. She brought the can over to his bed and laid out its contents. His stock consisted of two unlabeled pill bottles, five concert ticket stubs, a butane lighter, 1¼-inch rolling papers, a half-empty tube of model glue, a matchbook from a strip club in Peabody, and an envelope of cash. Jayne returned all but the bank and tucked the envelope in the waistband of her jeans for the few steps to her room.

She ate two slices of toast with peanut butter in the kitchen and got set for school. The breakfast would hold her until she returned to the apartment, because she tended to avoid the lunchroom on days Émile's schedule didn't align with her own. The cafeteria was a large, brash microcosm of society she generally chose not to find a seat in. Kids paired with one group or another after elementary school, but Jayne preferred to choose her few friends from among the whole populace.

She took a moment to wipe the kitchen counter. She hoisted her two hardcover, paper bag-sleeved books onto her hip to leave. A draft of chilly air streamed through the seams of the front door and gave Jayne a hint of the temperature on the other side. Michael's orphaned jacket hung on the wall. She plucked the lined denim jacket from its hook, and it engulfed her upper body, hanging to mid-thigh. She folded the cuffs to free her hands and pulled the jacket closed, feeling a sense of comfort from Michael's scent. She locked the door and traversed the icy walk.

Once on Market Street, she walked beside slow-moving traffic. The sidewalk was not clear and made foot travel hazardous. Soon she would reach the high school and again be ensconced as one with the masses. A clatter and crush of people in the corridors allowed her the feel of near invisibility as long as the cousins were not in range. It was on first bell that she left her locker and walked in a shallow stream of anxiety to the classroom.

CHAPTER SIX

Jayne eased up her stride in front of the Skillet Bar. She felt a sensation of pins and needles climb up the back of her neck in nervous excitement. At the entrance, tied open with a cord, was a black wrought iron gate, made of the same iron bar that secured the small windows at either side. She reached for the heavy wood door within and pulled it open. She let her eyes adjust to the low-light conditions to take in a familiar interior as the door closed of its own volition behind her back.

Dark wainscoting traveled the perimeter of the long, narrow room below a tin ceiling. At her feet lay a reclaimed-wood floor, nailed in place at the time of the last mill closures. Two large, framed mirrors hung behind the bar. They provided patrons with a semblance of company and a call for reflection. The bar ran down the length of the room and ended in a left curve to the wall.

Michael had introduced Jayne to the proprietor, Galen Stathakis, after his prior arrest, when he was out on bail and before his court date. Galen was a big man with thick, meaty hands and black hair that ran above his ears to the back of his head, the locks that remained at his age tied back with a small band, and short curls hung to his collar.

Michael had brought her by, and Galen shook her hand as if the young girl before him was an adult, with a grip that was firm and lasting. She would learn that the gesture was not one he ever proffered to strangers.

The three gathered in a booth. Michael nudged Jayne's elbow for her to pay attention and to scoot over to allow him more room. At first,

Galen railed against Michael's missteps. But their discussion was soon peppered with laughter while she took in her surroundings, daydreaming as the
men imbibed alcohol. Michael and Galen reminisced about Galen's friendship with their father, Terry. And Jayne's ears perked up at his name. She
listened closely to tales of past troubles on the Common. Lore of legendary
violent battles over ethnic and territorial lines. Being young, the discussion
gave Jayne insight into her neighborhood. An understanding she would never have come to at home. And words on a father who was lost to them years
ago. She liked to think her mother was different back then, kinder when he
was alive. But she knew otherwise. Some people were simply not meant to
raise children.

    In a promise to Michael, Jayne visited Galen once a month. The
man provided her with money for needs not met by their mother, and Michael worked off the debt upon his release. That was the old arrangement.
Since Michael had returned to the streets, Jayne steered clear of the Skillet.
Her brother dropped her a few dollars every few weeks or left it with the janitor at the high school when unwilling or unable to swing by the apartment.

    Jayne had not seen Galen in over a year, and she realized, standing
before him now, that she should have appreciated his help more. She missed
the big man. He sat on a far stool, likely aware of Jayne's presence. He read
the city newspaper with his eyeglasses perched low on his nose. And Jayne
stood and waited, working out her plan of approach. She felt small, uncer-
tain of the greeting she would receive.

    New England winters isolated many, and in her loneliness, she un-
derstood the lure of a bar. A place for people to gather to connect or to sit
with others in a shared space.

    In from the back hall walked a long-haired, thin-waisted man in
jeans and a loose black jersey, his sleeves pushed up to his elbows and a
brown leather band tied around his wrist. He carried a case of beer and met
Jayne's expectant expression with a frown. When he turned his head to set

down the beer, Jayne saw the man's scar that began at the corner of his left eye and swung down his cheek in a half moon, missing the corner of his mouth by a hair.

"You lost?" he asked.

"No. Why? Do I look lost?" Jayne thrust her hands into the pockets of Michael's jacket and made her way down to stand by Galen's stool. "Hey, Galen. Got a minute?"

Galen abandoned his paper and set down his eyeglasses on the bar. He looked Jayne over, head to toe. "Michael get himself hung up again?"

Jayne shrugged, knowing in her gut the question was rhetorical.

Galen gestured with his chin to the same booth they'd sat in on her first visit. He stood and lifted an index finger from the bar. "Set me up, Tao. It's that time of day."

Jayne and Galen stepped over and eased into the bench seats as Tao approached. He set down a shot glass of ouzo in front of Galen and returned behind the bar with nary a glance. With faint hope of service, Jayne cut to the chase. She reached for the inside pocket of Michael's jacket and slid her brother's offering across the table.

Galen pulled cash from the envelope and counted it out. "There's four hundred here. You're two bills short."

"I'm not short anything. Michael's short. And he got picked up yesterday."

"And sent you as his emissary," he said, getting his meaning across with few words. Galen looked down at Jayne's hands, and his features softened at the sight of an obvious tremor. He reached across the table and placed one of his large, warm hands over hers. "You're too young to have your mother's affliction. I don't still make you nervous, do I, Jayne?"

She leaned back and pulled her hand free. "No."

Galen tipped his shot back. He upended the glass and set it down on the table, a touch too hard, causing Jayne to jump. "I'm guessing Margaret's the cause of that bruise on your cheek," he said.

Jayne tested the tenderness of the skin with the tips of two fingers. The well-used concealer she had applied in the morning had long ago worn off, and the age of the hurt was showing its true colors.

"She ever do any real damage? Anything you can't handle?"

Jayne shook her head once and looked over to the bar for a moment of respite. She met Tao's cold appraisal. The bartender rested his backside on the shelf under the bar's offerings and refused to break his stare.

"Damn," Jayne whispered, surprised by his hard expression.

Galen held up a finger off the table, and Jayne waited in silence. She picked at a groove in the Formica with her thumbnail until a second shot glass arrived.

"You two have great communication skills," she said at Tao's departure.

"Tao is city-born, just like you. He traveled a bit, but he found his way back home." His lips rose in a smile of amusement, and he leaned back in the seat. "He gets me." Galen reached into the chest pocket of his shirt for what could only be a phantom pack of cigarettes. "How're you getting by? Anyone besides your mother causing you problems?"

"No."

The door to the bar opened, and a glare fanned out on the floor. A stout man, scruffy, peeked in and removed his cap. He looked at Tao.

"Not now," Tao said.

The man shrugged and let the door close as he stepped back out onto the sidewalk.

"What's with our friend this afternoon?" Galen said.

"Got into a fight with Suzanne's dumb-as-a-brick boyfriend last Friday. I had to heave them both out by the neck." Tao stood up straight and reached for a pen. "I told Brendan not to come back till he repents," he said, placing the pen behind his ear.

"Repents how?"

Tao shrugged. "Got me. But I'm thinking of absolving him tomorrow. Get caught up with his latest crazy idea."

Galen laughed and glanced back at Jayne. "How old are you now?"

"Sixteen."

"You look twelve, thirteen, tops."

"Nothing I can do about that," she said, crossing her arms on the table. She tugged with her thumb and first finger on the arm of Michael's jacket.

"You work?" he asked.

"Nope. I filled out an application for a job stocking shelves last summer, but Margaret put a nix on that. She wouldn't sign paperwork for me."

"How about a driver's license."

"Nope."

Galen nodded and set his hands flat and wide on the table.

"Why you taking an interest?" she asked. "Michael reach out to you already or something?"

"No, but seeing as we have a debt to square, I thought you'd come work for me."

"Here? In the bar?"

"No—out on the streets. But not the way it sounds."

"Not grasping the 'Michael's bet being my debt' part, but I'm interested if you're seriously offering me a job." The thought alone sparked a flicker of confidence in Jayne, and it felt good.

"I'll lay the details out when you come back tomorrow," he said, scratching over the pocket on his shirt. "And Jayne, let me tell that mother of yours."

Jayne considered Galen's reply as parting words and scooted out of the booth with a nod of assent. On her way to the door, she lifted her

chin and challenged Tao's stoic expression. "Smile, man. God loves you."
Jayne pushed open the heavy door and stepped out into the frigid air. She
walked under the red and orange hues thrown afar by the setting sun with
butterflies doing a merry dance in her stomach.

CHAPTER SEVEN

Jayne rested her head down on her forearms for the tail end of last period study hall being held in a section of the library. At the bell, she gathered up her things and walked out between tall swinging doors. She headed down the hall as students hustled to their lockers and headed for the exits.

Jayne swung down a wide set of stairs to the basement. She entered the school's supply room and approached Mr. Grover. He was sitting on a metal stool at a table in the corner. On seeing Jayne, he reached over to his cart and pulled off a long piece of duct tape from a roll on the cart's handle. The veins on the back of his hand were pronounced and led up a sleeve of long underwear that poked from beneath his blue coveralls. He reached out and cut the length of tape with a utility knife before holding the strip in his outstretched hand. Jayne grabbed the end with a smile and lifted her boot up to rest on a rung of a nearby stool. She wound the tape around the toe of her boot over remnants of a previous piece. The fix sealed a crack in the rubber for her short walk home. She nodded her thanks and made her way to an exit leading to the parking lot.

She had a destination today. And a job that would take her away from reruns of *Gomer Pyle* and *F Troop*. On a normal day, she sat in the living room and ate whatever she was able to throw together for dinner. She watched television and shared space on the couch with Margaret before heading to her room. Lately, it was the only time she spent with her mother.

She reached the apartment after a brisk walk, her face reddened by the wind and strands of her hair hanging out of her loosened braid. She fixed herself a bowl of cereal and stood next to the sink as she ate. Jayne felt an energy about her new way forward. An eagerness to begin walking whatever road she had started down. She washed her dish, cleaned herself up in the bathroom, and pulled Michael's jacket from the back of the chair in the kitchen to start back toward the bar.

≈

Jayne stood inside the door of the Skillet. A haze of smoke hung in the air around her, suspended in the meager rays of sun let in by small rectangles of stained glass on each side of the door.

Four customers sat at the bar. Two of them argued over the worth of a freshman relief pitcher acquired by the Red Sox. Tao lifted a bottle from the shelf and gave it a swipe of a wet cloth. He glanced at Jayne's reflection in one of the mirrors before setting down the bottle and aggressively flinging the white towel in his hand to the sink under the taps. He rounded the bar and seemed to eat up the floor between them as he rapidly approached.

Jayne consciously blinked twice. "Galen's expecting me," she said.

Tao moved back only a step and stood fast.

Jayne craned her neck. She peered around his body at chest level. "The boss man in or what?"

"I'll cover Michael's debt until he pops his head up," Tao responded as if no question was posed. "Until then—don't want you in here. Now skedaddle on back across the road, little one." He gestured with his chin to the front door.

Jayne straightened her spine with resolve. She was determined to hold on to the newfound confidence from the previous day, precarious though it may be. "I'm here to see Galen."

"Not wise. Listen to what I'm offering."

She rolled her eyes and mimicked his stance by crossing her arms over her chest. "Do you mind not being such a drag? I don't know you from Adam. And I didn't ask you for nothing."

Tao slowly and reluctantly stepped aside after what appeared to be careful contemplation. "Suit yourself. He's in his office."

Jayne unbuttoned Michael's jacket as she made her way to the back hallway. She knocked on the door around the corner from the men's room and glanced back over her shoulder. Galen called out, and Jayne entered the room. She closed the door when prompted and took a seat on the small leather couch across from his desk.

"Sweet, sweet Jayne. You've returned," Galen said. He pushed paperwork to the side of his desk and leaned back in his swivel chair.

"What's up with your bartender running interference?" she said.

"Tao?" Galen smiled and glanced for a moment at the office door. "He's not keen on me corrupting minors. I told him he could give saving your soul a shot. Don't let him scare you." He lifted his hand and adjusted the eyeglasses. "That being said—you're to show him and me respect. I can see testing limits and boundaries, but always keep in mind who I am to those around me. Out there—think before you speak."

"Jeez Louise."

Galen frowned. He reached into the side drawer of his desk, pulled out a rubber band, and stretched it over a stack of bills by the phone. He swiveled and stowed the money in a safe behind him with a sound of protest from the chair's springs. "Enter from the rear door from now on. I don't want the heat seeing your underage ass coming and going. Most days it's unlocked until I leave for the night." Galen turned back to his desk. "If you need in late—you call the bar phone."

"What will I be doing?"

"You, girl, are to be my runner. I need eyes and ears out there. A little mouse I can let loose to gather those tidbits of information I need to handle my business."

"Why me?"

"Why not? This arrangement can work for all of us. Michael included."

Jayne nodded, satisfied with Galen's short reply.

"Tao's going to be your keeper the next few days. He's to make the introductions. Get you on your feet," he said. Galen pulled his chair on caster wheels to the side of the desk. He opened the door and whistled one strong note. He rolled back, pushed his glasses farther up his nose, and tented his hands.

Tao arrived through the office door as he pulled on a worn leather jacket. A striped scarf hung from his neck and reached past his waist. "She ready for me?"

Galen reached into his desk drawer and extracted a satchel. He threw it to Tao, who caught it with one hand at his waist. Galen leaned back and set his hands on the arms of his chair. "She'll soon learn how much to carry to complete the rounds. For now, there's enough cash there for our man downtown. You're to meet him outside the Owl Diner in ten minutes. I don't want you depending on collections while you're showing our *pontiki* here the route."

Tao smiled and surprised Jayne with the change in his demeanor. A 180 since her arrival.

Galen returned Tao's grin. He pulled a slip of paper from his pocket and extended his hand. "I'll need to know from you how she interacts with our people. I trust you to gauge for yourself if she's up to the job." Galen patted his palm over his breast pocket. "Pick up a book bag she can use on the runs—not from army/navy, but one that will hold up just as good. And Tao—don't get any ideas. Keep to the whores. Got it?"

Tao expelled a quick cough of a laugh. "Kid's way too skinny for me, boss."

"What the heck?" Jayne said. "Can we just hit the road, Jack?"

Tao stepped back and gestured with his hand for Jayne to lead the way out of the building. They left through the rear door and walked down the long alley. Jayne soon lagged a step behind in a jerky cadence in an attempt to keep up with Tao's strides.

His truck sat in one of the few cleared spots on the street. He opened the passenger door and stood back on a snowbank to let Jayne pass under his arm.

She lifted herself awkwardly into the seat as he closed the heavy door, saving her from the brisk wind. As he walked to the driver's side, she looked to the front, side, and rear of the vehicle. She scanned the sidewalk for a chair, garbage can, or sawhorse. "You going to put something down to save your space?" she asked as he settled in the seat and started the engine.

"Nah. Jimmy Tens is coming by with the plow. He'll clear a few spaces. Worst comes to worst, I can ride up over the bank."

"Cool." She could feel the diesel engine's low hum in her belly. She shivered briefly from the cold and watched as Tao rubbed his hands together.

They waited together a few minutes for the engine to warm. He tapped a knuckle on the heater vent and pulled out of the space with little difficulty. He made a U-turn toward the diner and their first stop on the run.

A short drive down the road and Tao pulled the truck up beside a late-model sedan that idled in front of a converted boxcar. Tao got out and gestured to Jayne with his head to follow. She exited the high cab of the truck with an awkward stumble from miscalculating the distance to the ground.

The driver of the car turned and braced his forearm on the back of the seat as Tao followed Jayne into the back of the car. The man wore a bulky gold watch, and a small black cuff link secured the sleeve of his dress shirt under a dark blue suit coat.

"This here is Jayne. Our new collector," Tao said.

"Howdy, Jayne."

Tao opened the zipper of the satchel and passed over an open envelope of cash. "Same terms as last time, same schedule. You want her meeting you here?"

"No. Have her come by the office. My secretary will have the payments ready. Just as long as she doesn't need to go counting it out in front of her."

Tao shook his head. "Not necessary. Seal the damn things. Word of caution, though—don't go sending it light. He's going to trust his girl over you."

The man gave Jayne a curious look.

Tao turned his head in her direction. "First lesson of the day. So, listen close. Never get in a car. You're here because I'm in here with you. Capisce?"

Jayne nodded and fiddled nervously with the cover of a small ashtray on the armrest of the door.

Tao tapped her knee with a knuckle. "I don't care whose car it is. You ride with me or Jimmy Tens. That's it. Most days you'll be hoofing it, and stops will be two minutes, tops. Dress warm so you're not tempted. Understand?"

Jayne nodded, and Tao reached across her to open the door. They both left the vehicle and approached the different sides of the truck. Jayne lifted herself up again, by the grab handle over the window this time. She looked over to Tao as he put the truck in gear and reversed out into the street.

"What?" he asked.

"You don't know me. Why would you say you trusted me?"

"You need better hearing. Galen trusts you. He wouldn't have taken you on if he didn't. I trust his judgment. Out here—always use conviction in your words. They need to believe what you tell them, when you tell them. Otherwise, they don't have to do jack shit. And they'll think they can take advantage. We've … *I've* got your back. And you'll have my support until Galen says otherwise."

Jayne leaned back in the bench seat and turned her head. She glanced out the window and looked at the dirt and grime already marring the snowbanks after the recent storm. For a moment she caught sight of a man who waited far too long to shovel out his car. He battled aggressively with the hard, ice-encrusted snowbank with only an Irish spade, a garden shovel ill-suited to the task.

≈

As the last vestige of the sun descended, Tao pulled the truck into the parking lot of Zayre's department store. They had managed four stops and had four similar interactions, a new contact made for Jayne at each location.

Jayne was tired. She felt a weariness in her limbs as she followed Tao down the aisles. He pushed a cart and glanced back at her occasionally, but seemingly only to gauge her size as he gathered up two sweatshirts, a rain slicker with a hood, and two pairs of mittens.

"What's all this stuff? Thought we were here for a bag," she said.

Tao steered down the next aisle and reached for a book bag with a thick, adjustable strap that could be pulled across the body. He held it up in the air and turned over the tag.

"No way," she said.

"Why not?"

"It has fringe."

"So?"

Jayne extended an arm out in emphasis. "Friiiinge."

Tao reached out and grabbed a replacement. The bag had the same thick strap but was without the offensive trim. It sported a small bear paw, embossed by the zipper. The detail was understated and suited Jayne. The bag had seams that were double-stitched, and the bottom was reinforced. He placed his find on top of the other items and pushed the cart toward the front of the store. "Tomorrow we stop near the train station for boots. You have a winter coat other than the rag hanging off your shoulders?"

Jayne pulled Michael's jean jacket around her body more tightly. "I've got a coat."

≈

On the last errand of the run, one for the bar, Jayne stayed in the warmth of the truck cab as Tao entered McKittrick's Hardware on Fletcher Street. He had left the engine running, and she became relaxed enough to yawn and rest her eyes for a spell.

She was looking forward to the coming days working for Galen. It would be a far cry from an after-school existence of walking with friends to the river, being holed up in her room after dinner waiting for Margaret to go to bed, or exploring the far corners of the city with no destination in mind.

She would pull Michael's old bicycle down from the wall in the back hall of the apartment when the weather grew warm. She would travel the routes they gave her without the need to hop a bus or trouble either man for a ride. Life experience with her mother had made her independent, and she strived to keep it that way. If the bicycle chain fell off, she would put it back on. If she had a flat tire, she would wipe the inner tube with soapy water to find the escaping air. She would scrape the surface over the leak to adhere a seal and wheel it over to Macheras Service Mart for air. She would do what needed to be done to grow confidence in herself. And, saints willing, pride from others.

CHAPTER EIGHT

Tao exited the hardware store and made his way back to the truck. He pulled Jayne's feet down from his glove compartment and startled her awake. "I'm dropping you home now. Get plenty of sleep, because our list of stops will be longer tomorrow. Payday for the working man, so collections will triple."

She straightened her back against the seat and glanced out the side window.

Tao kept his arms down by his sides. "When you're out on your own, on any of the stops—you have someone asking to place a bet or wants to do business other than what you're there for—you tell them to screw. Keep a roll of dimes with you. And learn fast where the phone booths are. Because you're going to be calling in often. They're your lifeline. Got a question, you call. See something hinky, you call. Rely on your instincts and call in, even when it's quiet."

Jayne nodded.

"And change up the route. No five afternoons at the same phone, same time. I'll teach you how to mix it up as you go along," he said.

She stifled a yawn, and her eyes watered.

Tao tapped her knee with a knuckle. "Me or Galen will pick up—every time. And we don't want to have to track your little behind down. We'll guide you until we're confident you're making the decisions we would make."

"What?" she asked.

"We're going to be all on the same page. No missteps, no stumbling around in the dark."

"All right, all right."

"I know you're tired. We'll talk tomorrow before we head out." Tao shrugged out of his leather jacket and dropped it behind the bench seat. "I'm going to find a marker, something to leave at the back door. It'll be our signal for you to steer clear of the bar. Something to warn you. If we have company and need you to hang back."

Jayne sat forward and adjusted one of the packages leaning against her leg. "When do I get to fly solo?"

"We're stuck together until Galen says otherwise." He put the truck in gear, pulled out of the lot, and drove up the street with traffic. After hitting his blinker to take a right at the next set of lights, he rapped on the dash to settle the sputter of the heating fan. He wished he had tinkered with the mechanism earlier in the season. The concern with keeping the slight girl beside him warm came as a surprise.

$\approx$

In the morning, Tao backed his truck out of his driveway and drove to the Acre, Lowell's toughest neighborhood. His destination was a group of units at O'Brien Terrace. He parked his truck and slouched down to rest, his eyes trained on an apartment door.

Tao had experience with the day-to-day poverty of the inhabitants. He had never lived at O'Brien Terrace himself, but he knew of the struggles. Income was the consideration on being allotted a place in the development run by the city housing authority. For most years, Tao's family would have qualified for the long waiting list kept for occupancy.

He was born at Saint Joseph's Hospital up the road in 1949 and was raised in the Highlands off Stevens Street in a house where money was indeed scarce. Tao still managed to retain memories of a happy childhood, though, even with a father who was frequently volatile and temperamental.

David Mann worked construction, often a seasonal occupation. He bore the leather skin of a man exposed to the outdoors on a regular basis, his hands rough with calluses. Hard skin he trimmed with a knife at the kitchen table. His temper was short, and he found pleasure in gambling, despite the wins being few and far between.

On the weekends, when Tao's father wasn't out fixing the family car, the only car, he wore out the newspaper. He studied horses and jockeys that were running and results of the previous day as he drank an endless cup of tea. He studied basketball and baseball lineups and injury rosters. Tao's mother and father never discussed money in front of their children. Never worried aloud about the future or days ahead. Because what was, was. And the start of an argument between the two was the start of a series of long, silent, stressful days.

Tao had known the Greek since the day Tao turned twelve years old. Since the first time he was sent to the Skillet to settle one of his father's debts. Those visits became a regular occurrence. They saved his old man a long walk to the end of the bar.

Tao was a smart kid. He was aware of the sacrifices his family made in support of his father's vice. There were dinners of canned beans and slices of fried bologna. Days when condiments were the meat of a sandwich, often sliced cheese with mustard. Nights a couple times a month when his mother would cook a large pot of rice pudding on the stove for dinner. A sprinkle of cinnamon, and Tao was happy. He ate as many bowls as he could manage, and on those nights, he went to bed with a full stomach.

As a boy, he learned to read the air. He was ready when his father went off like a shot at the mere hint of unpleasant news or on the direction of the wind. He witnessed weeks his father walked in shadow even on bright sunny days. But from an early age, Tao realized his father worked to the bone for each paycheck—long, hard, grueling days. And Tao believed deep down to his soul that his dad deserved all the fleeting pleasures he got out of gambling, believed the man's responsibilities ended with a roof over their heads and food on the table. And even though they only scraped by, his father delivered, and his father stayed.

Tao coped with any uncertainties and fears for his family by gathering around him a tight-knit group of friends. And they explored: from simple hunts for salamanders in moist, dark soil, to games of capture the flag and pickup games of all manner, whether they possessed the right equipment or not, fights to pass the time and add life to a dull afternoon, shoplifting excursions on a dare or when they ran low on candy bars or cigarettes, swimming in the Merrimack and jumping from one of the lower bridges.

School days filled up the rest of Tao's time, a worthy distraction that kept him and his cohorts out of juvenile hall. And after the streetlights came on and they pushed for another hour or two of play, he and his friends meandered home for the night to rest up for the next day's adventure.

By eighteen, he was an easygoing, gangly kid who slept in the same twin bed at his parents' house that he had slept in at ten years old, his feet dangling off the edge most nights. Tao's mother aged gracefully over the years, a few gray hairs at the temple, a few pounds around her waist. But his father's appearance changed markedly. The masonry jobs David Mann took on led to a permanent stoop in his posture. Stress-related injuries to his body mounted, and the man grew tired right before their eyes. Fortunately, his gambling habit also dissipated in degrees. It was reduced to a couple bets a month on Boston teams and a road trip down to Baltimore with a coworker, Larry, to the Pimlico racetrack for the Preakness.

Tao registered for selective service. He discovered he was blessed with a birthdate and initials that kept him out of the draw the following year. Kept him out of the draw in two lotteries that could have sent him to fight in the Southeast Asian conflict. College held little appeal, with its cost and structured norms, but Tao read books by science fiction authors Stanislaw Lem and Robert A. Heinlein, books by men of the Beat generation.

And the words of hometown boy Jack Kerouac, who on the rare occasion could be seen around town in the company of Father Spike. Tao read the prose of Ken Kesey. Writings that served to fill him with wanderlust.

He hitchhiked his way to the lower tip of the Great Lakes and managed to pick up one long ride with a truck driver who drove up through the southern border of Canada and out to the West Coast. The man spoke French, and the two exchanged a total of four stilted sentences on their journey.

For a year and two months, Tao remained in California. He first lasted three grueling days picking raspberries in San Mateo beside migrants who made a meager wage merely to survive hand to mouth. Tao could barely sit the third day without the immediate impulse to scream out in pain. He put his thumb to use again and traveled the road farther south. He hooked up with an outfit as temporary labor on construction sites, feeling a visceral connection to his father in the work, even without contact with by phone or post.

His expectations of fulfillment were dashed in only a few short months, and a malaise slowly took hold. Each week that passed led to more of a struggle to get up from under an oppressive funk, until, down the lane, a particularly bad trip on acid provided Tao with a revelation, a spark of realization. No matter how far he traveled or how carefully chosen a place was to settle, he would inherently remain the same person; only the scenery changed. Within the week, he pulled up loose stakes and made the long journey home.

The time away was fruitful, though. It gave him insight into human nature from the many interactions he had along the way, and his instincts grew sharp. He was fortunate to be one to catch on quick to people's motivations. The talent proved to be a time-saving art in Galen Stathakis's employ.

It was on his return that Galen offered him the job as bartender at the Skillet, an occupation he took to immediately. With the position, he gained a friend and a mentor. Tao had grown into a man. A man who was hesitant to pass judgment and long on patience. He had the perfect makeup of a great bartender, and his loyalty to Galen made him indispensable.

Galen was impressed, and to anchor Tao further, he offered the money for first, last, and deposit to rent a house a mere three streets over from Tao's own parents.

≈

Jayne Ranney's appearance on the stoop before him dashed Tao's recollections and brought him to attention as she exited the apartment. She locked the dead bolt behind her as she held open the storm door with a hip. Her new book bag sat balanced upright between her legs on the concrete slab. Jayne turned as she pulled her braided hair out from her collar and stepped to the walkway. He tapped once on the truck horn and rolled down his window as she veered over in his direction.

She reached within a stone's throw of Tao's window, hoisted her bag farther over her right shoulder, and pushed her hands deep into the pockets of her jacket.

"Why aren't you wearing a pair of the mittens we picked up yesterday?" Tao asked.

"I'm in high school, not third grade. They make me feel silly."

Tao shook his head in disapproval. "I need your keys. You can grab them from me later."

"What for?"

"A chat with your mother. I don't want to have to jimmy the lock."

She glanced at the apartment door before turning back and dropping her eyes to the pavement between her feet. "You don't really need to talk to her, do you?"

Tao tapped his palm twice on the truck door. "Gimme here."

Jayne tossed him her keys after hesitating and made her way to Market Street. Tao watched from his side-view mirror as she slowed over a patch of black ice that had glazed the path overnight and as she moved to the snowy edge of the walk to reach the street.

He waited until Jayne was out of sight before leaving his truck and unlocking the front door to the apartment. He entered with little effort to conceal his presence. Attempting to sneak into an unfamiliar space with an occupant wholly unaware was idiotic and rife for misunderstanding.

The layout before him was simple. A narrow set of concrete stairs with a metal banister for a handrail led to a second floor. They were building materials generally used for stairs in commercial construction, more at home in an industrial warehouse or basement area of a municipal building. In the living room sat a green couch on a burnt-orange area rug. A coffee table, low and dark, was polished to a shine but peppered with burn marks on two of its edges. A square-block lamp sat on a side table beside a glass ashtray, the corners in perfect line with its base. The kitchen, a floor of tan and white linoleum squares, transitioned from the living room with no dividing wall. The kitchen was clean and its counters clear but for one knife and a small dish drying on a rack by the sink. There was a hint of lemon in the air.

Tao walked a few steps to the refrigerator and, to feed his curiosity, opened the door and scanned its sparse contents. On the top of the refrigerator sat an open carton of cigarettes and to the right, in a narrow cabinet, sat two twin bottles of vodka with both of their seals cracked for convenience.

He walked over and made his way up the stairs to the second floor. He passed two open bedroom doors before pausing at the far one, from which silence reigned. He opened the door and took a moment to take in a scene of utter disarray.

Margaret Ranney lay under a bedspread patterned with a design of bright, gargantuan flowers. The woman's blond hair, betrayed by brown roots, flowed over her pillow and effectively concealed her face. On a night-stand, cigarette butts sat suspended in a glass of briny liquid. Other butts were tamped down and overflowed from a blue candy dish that sat precariously on the window shelf. The heavy blinds on the window were nearly drawn. Clothes and used towels were scattered on the floor. A full-size mirror hung from the back of the closet door, and an iron sat on top the dresser. The appliance emitted a low electrical hum.

He unplugged the iron, flipped on the light switch, and inadvertently kicked a glass by his foot. It rolled, clattering across the floorboards, before coming to rest under the bed.

"Christ," Margaret said as she lifted her head.

"Try again. I'm doubtful the second coming's planned for this neck of the woods."

Margaret sat upright and rubbed one of her heavy-lidded eyes. "What's going on? Jayne let you in?"

"Jayne's at school, Mrs. Ranney." Tao moved closer and tugged the covers down to the end of the bed. "Now move your tush. We need to get you in the shower."

She reached desperately for the bedspread at her feet. "Stay away from me."

"Nope. Need you awake. Awake and aware." He caught her under the arm and propelled her small frame to the door.

She leaned her weight to the side and tugged in a failed attempt to break free. He ignored her effort and dragged her down the hall, down the stairs, and over to the bathroom. He pushed open the door with the outer side of his foot. He pulled back the shower curtain and, with his free hand, turned on the water.

Margaret's struggles only tightened his hold, and he forced her forward, over the lip of the tub. She stood under the water clothed in a long

T-shirt and the pair of mismatched socks she appeared to have worn to bed.

"I'll go make coffee. Take the time to get in your right mind and come meet me in the kitchen," he said.

Margaret pulled aside strands of wet hair that were plastered in front of her eyes. "What the hell are you doing here?"

Tao ignored her. He left the bathroom, leaving the door ajar. He located a jar of Taster's Choice instant coffee in the cupboard above the sink and heated water in a small pot on the stove. He used a finger to wipe a thin layer of dust off the lid of the jar.

She arrived after a few minutes dressed in a bathrobe he had seen hanging from the back of the bathroom door. Her hair was brushed and clipped back from her face. She grabbed a pack of cigarettes and a lighter from the carton up high. She eased down into a chair at the table and stared at Tao as she lit up her cigarette and inhaled a healthy hit of nicotine.

He poured water over the large grains of coffee he had spooned into two mugs, stirred the contents, and set one down on the table. "As you know, there's no milk. Black it is."

"I don't do coffee." She sat back in the chair, her arms crossed, her lips set in a straight, tense line.

"Drink it," he said.

Margaret rolled her eyes in frustration and took a sip. "Happy?"

"No. All of it. Down the hatch."

She rested her lit cigarette on the table edge. She lifted the mug with both hands and swallowed three large gulps. She set it down and breathed in deep through her nose before all color washed from her face. Pale to begin with, it was a sight to behold.

"Oh, God," she said. Margaret stood from the table and lunged for the sink. She vomited up the coffee before performing a series of dry heaves. Her knuckles were white as she gripped the countertop. She rinsed her mouth with tap water, dried her hands on a towel tucked into the handle of the silverware drawer, and wiped sweat from her brow. She stepped over and reached a trembling hand out to the table for her cigarette. "Any other bright ideas, you ugly bastard?"

Tao's upper lip lifted in a smirk without compunction. "Weak stomach?"

"Bite me," she said.

"Do you know who I am?"

"You work for the Greek."

He nodded.

"What's he want with me?" She pulled down an ashtray. She stubbed out her cigarette and wasted no time in lighting a replacement. "You going to tell me why you're here, or not? The Greek running for office or something?"

"Galen found work for your daughter, Jayne, after school. And a couple morning or afternoon hours on the weekends."

"Good for her. Again, what's he want with me?"

"To make sure this arrangement causes Jayne no problems here at home."

"Nice of him."

"Cut the shit." Tao took a sip of his coffee that had been warming his hand and poured the rest down the sink. "I caught sight of those fading bruises, same as Galen. And I'd like nothing better than to throw you up against that wall and choke you out." He leaned back on the counter and sighed. "But for now, I'm to impress upon you Galen's fondness for the girl and the ramifications of you taking light of that fact. You have a heavy hand when it comes to disciplining her. Or whatever reason it is you give yourself to strike her. And it will no longer be tolerated."

Margaret blew smoke toward the ceiling. A slow smile formed on her face. "You look like you'd be right at home hanging at Mother's. Wasting daylight with the other derelicts. But you talk like some highfalutin lawyer. You charging Galen by the hour?"

"Mother's shut their doors."

"Pity," she said, pointing to his cheek. "That from a knife fight in their parking lot?"

He ran his hand down the scar. "Not that it's any of your business, but I never visited the place. It was too frigging far down the road."

"You missed some good times then."

"I bet. Now, back to Jayne."

"I don't care what she does."

"Obviously," Tao said, glancing over at the clock on the living room wall.

Margaret set her cigarette on the side of the ashtray and stood. She pulled grape juice from the refrigerator and one of the twins from the cabinet.

If Tao's childhood memories proved accurate, the level of alcohol in Margaret's glass would rise over the course of the day. An uncle of his had convinced himself that juice was the cause not only of persistent heartburn, but also the chronic stomach pains he suffered through the years. The man eventually took to drinking the mass-produced vodka straight up and died of stomach cancer in '59.

Tao shook his head. "You clear on what I'm telling you about not hassling the kid? Verbally or physically?"

"Get it. Now get out. If Michael were here, you'd be crawling to the door."

"Lady, Michael's the reason Jayne came to us. You think Galen and I have an interest in looking after a teenage girl if we don't have to?"

"I just assumed you two wanted a piece."

Tao swore in disbelief as he zipped up his jacket. He made his way to the front door and reached out for the doorknob. "Clean that sink. If I hear you left a mess for her, I'll be back tomorrow for another round of lawyerly pontification." He left and locked the dead bolt. He pocketed the set of keys and made his way over to his truck. He would catch a couple hours of sleep at his house before heading in to work.

≈

Despite daytime being the harborage for regulars to the bar, one of the main aspects of Tao's job was to be vigilant, to follow conversation, keep a line on people, and analyze potential threats. He prided himself on his ability to read faces, posture, and intent. His observational skills provided Galen welcome relief from a constant state of alert.

The Skillet was only one of many establishments in Lowell that ran book, but Galen had feet planted on other corners in the underbelly of the city. Corners where the best course of conduct was a steady one, eyes wide open.

Galen settled into his seat at the bar before noon. He reviewed receipts and answered the phone by his side for the next few hours for a series of two-minute conversations. He adjusted himself on the stool periodically. His weight and sedentary state caused obvious discomfort to his lower back. Tao debated offering his boss a pill from the bottle of chalky white pain reliever under the register, but he had never known Galen to medicate himself, even with something as innocuous as Aspirin.

The front door opened, and Margaret Ranney entered, chin held high. She stopped a few feet from Galen and inhaled from her cigarette before blowing smoke off to the side.

Galen crossed his arms and leaned back on the stool. "You mind stepping back with that?"

She raised an eyebrow, threw her butt to the floor, and ground it out with the heel of her boot.

Brendan McHugh, the bar's resident Irishman, an émigré from ten years previous, passed behind her from the direction of the men's room.

He emitted a spontaneous, short burst of laughter. "Real classy, Peggy Sue."

"Shove it, Brendan." Margaret motioned with her hand to Tao. "Wolfschmidt, with ice."

Galen shook his head once, and Tao caught the movement in his peripheral vision.

"No can do," Tao said.

Margaret's eyes opened wide. "You denying me a drink in this dive?"

Galen sighed. "Just spit it out. What did you come in here to say to me?"

"I don't appreciate you sending your man here to my place. It was indecent."

The corner of Tao's upper lip rose in a way that reflected no humor. "Indecent? You abuse your own daughter. How decent is that?"

"Go straight to hell," she said.

"I'm confused. First, I'm the Messiah, and now…" Tao began.

Galen pushed the receipts forward on the bar and lowered his reading glasses. "Stay quiet for a minute, Tao. Let her finish."

Margaret switched her weight from one leg to the other and back. "I don't know what Jayne's doing for you, but she belongs home after school."

"You'd be best to manage on your own from now on," Galen said. He tapped his index finger on the bar.

Tao turned and grabbed the bottle of Ouzo off the shelf. He set a shot glass on the bar and poured.

"Fine," she said. She cocked her head to the side. "What you paying her?"

Galen raised his eyebrows. He removed his eyeglasses and set them down.

"I need to look out for my little girl," Margaret added.

Tao let out a laugh and set the ouzo bottle back on the shelf, a touch too hard. "Understatement of the year," he said.

Galen sighed and massaged his side with an open palm. "I've no patience today, Margaret. So, here's the skinny. You're not to take money from Jayne. Period. And if you lay another hand on that child, I won't be sending Tao. I'll be sending someone you don't recognize. Someone you'll see only once. Am I making myself clear?"

"Don't know why my Terry ever called you a friend," she replied.

Galen stood abruptly from his stool, causing the wooden legs to scrape the floor with a jarring sound.

She stumbled back in surprise and caught herself. She attempted poorly to project calm, reaching into her purse for a cigarette and lighter. It took three tries to accomplish the simple task of lighting her cigarette as her hands trembled. And with eyes cast down, she made her way out the front door.

In Tao's mind, her departure pulled a cloud of tension and negative energy from the bar.

Galen upended the shot down his throat before settling back in his seat.

Tao stared at the door and wistfully recalled Brendan's sage but curious advice: Be certain visitors left by the same door from which they came, and you keep dark spirits from lagging behind.

"Man, she's got mileage on her," Brendan said. He lifted his beer and brought it up to his lower lip. He was a Genesee man. "And so uncouth. It's nice to know you don't serve her lot in this fine establishment."

CHAPTER NINE

Two days of local detention, a perfunctory hearing, and Michael Ranney was processed into the Billerica House of Correction. He found the institutional drab-green walls of the past awash in color. The well-doers, those bastions of prison reform, had descended in his absence and involved the inmates in projects to beautify their surroundings.

Michael himself was a realist. Underneath the paint stood the same reinforced walls and cinder block. And the pretty patterns and artistic expressions of joy would soon fade, in all ways, to become cloying and as mentally confining as gray and green.

He reestablished all manner of connections. He became stocked with contraband from a new source and reacclimated to tier two in an assigned two-man cell. It took much longer to become desensitized to his cellmate's pervasive body odor. A man with more hair on his back than his head.

"Hey, Lenny, I'll give you two tailor-mades if you take a shower, man. You said yourself—your account in the commissary is shot," Michael said. He had a steady supply of cigarettes from a prison guard Galen procured as a courier. The arrangement gave Michael the ability to barter with the men. Many, cash-poor, stooped to smoking a harsh, lung-tearing alternative constructed piecemeal from cigarette butts. The leavings were rolled in available paper, and the sticks were constantly wet with spit to slow the burn.

Leonard Smith, serving a sentence of two and a half years, rolled over on the top bunk and emitted a spate of loud, noxious gas. "Ten."

"Five."

Lenny nodded, and Michael dropped the cigarettes into Lenny's hand. Michael stood from his bunk and took the two steps to empty his bladder. He held back the urge to physically lay into the Viking, knowing a trip to the infirmary for his roommate would be a temporary fix. Michael had too many balls in the air to be spending full days in solitary or run the risk of being transferred to a more secure facility.

After relieving himself, Michael rested back on his bunk and let his thoughts meander to the future, to the rolling months on the horizon. Galen would keep him busy at the prison with dealing, keeping book, and relaying messages of information or intimidation. Still, Michael would need a distraction. He was too hard, and hard-pressed, to remain celibate for an extended stretch. He was different from the prison wolves, though, because he was of the same persuasion inside as out. At Billerica, finding someone agreeable only took a cast of line in concrete waters.

≈

Michael huddled on a bench in his prison-issued coat and looked on in amusement as the new, tow-headed inmate walked into the yard. The young man had his eyes cast down to the ground in front of his feet. He moved under the basketball net, possibly on his way to the side fence.

A player twice the kid's size with the muscle mass and neck indicative of a weight lifter and the scars and misaligned nose of a fighter stopped play in the game. The beast glared as the target of his ire remained wholly unaware that darkness was a moment from descending.

Michael stood up from his seat on the edge of the court. He whistled a tone in the kid's direction using his thumb and first finger curled at the entrance of his mouth. "Hey, Tweety Bird. Over here."

The boy turned instantly as if the moniker was one bestowed on him at birth.

"You looking for trouble? You walked right through their field of play," Michael said with a smile.

The basketball game slowly resumed, the beast taking back up his position as a formidable guard at the top of the key. The boy swiped his palm over the bench to clean the seat and eased down to sit beside Michael.

Michael studied the demeanor of the recently initiated and motioned to the boy's split bottom lip. "What happened there, blondie?"

"Dinner—yesterday. Someone pushed me into the guy in front of me in line. And the bastard didn't even turn around. Just threw back a sharp elbow."

"Yup. Personal space's a currency here," Michael said. He extended his arm and shook the boy's hand. "Michael."

"Roy."

"How you finding things?"

"I'm not."

The two watched the rest of the game in silence and at a shout from a guard lined up with other inmates to head inside. Michael placed his hand on Roy's shoulder for a moment and felt a tap on his own from behind.

A low, grating voice spoke in his right ear. "You flush with weed?"

"Nah," Michael said.

He tilted his head to the side and away from the unwelcome, warm breath. "Hit me up on Tuesday."

≈

Michael and Roy met routinely in the yard and for meals. Michael passed on snippets of prison wisdom, locations of the best blinds, names of guards and inmates to avoid. He relayed tips on getting through a day unscathed. He built up Roy's confidence and taught him to walk with his head up, eyes forward. And the all-encompassing fear of harassment and abuse for the young man abated now that, through Michael, Roy was under the umbrella of the Greek's protection. Galen's name held weight and gravitas in Billerica. In truth, Galen's influence reached as far afield as Concord and Shirley.

Michael recalled the first time he himself was in jail and the vulnerable feelings that virginal incarceration instilled in him. It was analogous to a long drop into an ice-cold lake. Michael came up for air having no idea of the depth or the dangers that lurked below. He survived while feeling a baseline of fear as if he was treading water, limbs numb, body afloat in the cold. Galen stepped in after that first month, in deference to Michael's father, Terry. He eased Michael's stay.

In time, Roy too would relax and come to accept his new reality. And if his time was similar to the untold number before him, he would experience an emotional progression that would near guarantee a drop into a slow-settling state of depression.

Michael would be there to help him combat the malaise. Be there to break Roy out of any funk he might nestle himself into. It would be managed with talk of the future, talk of places to visit and things to do together when they hit the streets. It was a cruel tactic, in a way, because Michael had no intention of hooking up with Roy on the outside.

In cold resolve, he merely held fast to buoying Roy to a mindset where the boy was both useful and good company.

CHAPTER TEN

Tao Mann pulled his truck up opposite the high school. He peered through a windshield crusted in the corners with the remnants of ice, following his swift action with a windshield scraper in front of the bar. A late-season cold front had swooped down overnight and delivered a mix of frozen precipitation throughout the day. Tao idled the vehicle's engine and rested at the curb. He watched the entrance through a steady pelt of sleet for Jayne to appear.

Students streamed to buses parked in a long row. The cold caused clouds of exhaust from the bus tailpipes to billow out into the street. The weather made for slippery footing, and a few young men and women, poorly outfitted for the weather, found it difficult to remain upright, which provided Tao some amusement.

He spied Jayne making her way down the wide set of stairs. The hood of her sweatshirt covered her head, strands of hair trailed out at the collar, and the bulky denim jacket was wrapped tight around her body with both arms. Tao watched as a formidable boy with a slump to his wide shoulders broke from one of the lines to the buses and cut in Jayne's path, well before she reached the sidewalk. Her head lifted as if Tao had called out to her, and she acknowledged Tao's presence across the way with a nod. She turned her head a degree and up into the eyes of her impediment.

Tao saw frustration bloom on Jayne's face and witnessed her take a step back from the boy. He rolled down his window to catch the conversation, but their voices were indecipherable over the rumble of bus engines and the ambient noise from their fellow students. Wind-whipped sleet stung the side of Tao's face, and more rolled down the inside of the truck door in droplets from where it landed and melted. Tao cranked the pane closed with a curse and lay his hand on the door handle.

The boy turned his head, following Jayne's eyes as her attention landed back on the truck. The young man swung an arm out wide in query. Jayne veered around him after a few short words were exchanged. She walked across the road, checking each way for traffic as she crossed. Tao leaned over the bench seat and pushed open the passenger door. Jayne lifted herself up by the grab handle and sat with her book bag between her legs.

"What the hell was that?" he said.

"Who, Émile?" Jayne pulled back her hood and threaded wet fingers through her hair.

"He your boyfriend?" Tao asked.

"Nope."

"Jayne?"

"I haven't hung out with him for a while, and he wants to know where I've been."

"And?"

"And what? He's got no right to be pissy. What you doing here?"

Tao put the truck in gear and pulled away from the curb. "Galen has me picking up Chinese. Thought you might be hungry."

"What about my run?" She held her palms out over the vent on the dashboard.

"I took care of it," he said. "You can't be running around in this shit."

She looked over with surprise.

≈

Tao and Jayne sat at a booth in the bar of the Hong Kong in Chelmsford. Tao ordered them each a combination plate and the list of takeout items for Galen. The room was dim, light emanating from colorful pendant bulbs and a small black-and-white television that broadcast programming out of Boston.

Their waitress arrived back at the table and set down their drinks, a beer for Tao and ginger ale for Jayne.

"Anything else, honey?" she asked Tao.

"Hit me with another beer in a few minutes," Tao said.

Jayne took a long draw on her straw as the waitress, with an exaggerated swish of her hips, returned to the main room.

Tao leaned back in the booth and tilted his head to the side. "You keep yourself a mystery to that kid back at the school and he's going to keep at you."

"He asked who you were. What am I going to say?"

"Tell him I'm your mom's boyfriend or something."

Jayne snickered.

"What?"

"Last time Margaret brought a guy around, he had a stomach you could set that beer on and wore black socks with sandals."

"And way older, right?"

Jayne shrugged.

Tao lifted his beer and took a long pull on the bottle. "How've you been doing on your own?"

She lifted one shoulder. "Good."

"The bike of yours … Jimmy's fitting it with new tires today and giving it a once-over for when you can take it out. He wants to make sure it will get you by. Said something about it being too big for you."

"I'm keeping it."

"He'll see what he can do."

"How did he get it from the apartment? I swear it was there this morning."

"He's crafty. Your mother probably slept right through."

Jayne nodded.

Tao took another long pull of beer. "You're going to need to be careful getting around. Roads are a mess. They still have those beat-to-shit barrels breaking Merrimack into a two-way. Heaven knows how long before they get to all the goddamn potholes."

Jayne scooted forward on the seat. She sighed and pushed her drink cup closer to the middle of the table. "Wish the weather would get better."

Tao nodded. "How you getting on with Jimmy?"

She smiled for a moment in response. "You mean my shadow? I see him lurking at some of my stops. Yesterday he was out back of the school talking to Mr. Grover. Your man's got me peeking out my bedroom window when I can't sleep. I keep thinking he's there somewhere, sitting in his car in the dark."

Tao leaned back and raised an eyebrow. "Who's Mr. Grover?"

"The janitor. He knew my dad. Between classes or before school, if I'm early, I head down the basement. It's my spot. The noise gets too loud for me sometimes. And the halls are crowded. I take a few minutes to breathe in his office. Really—it's just a large closet with a couple chairs to sit on." Jayne glanced over to the bar and back over her shoulder at the approach to their booth. Seemingly satisfied, she opened her school bag at her hip. She pulled a slender, silver object out and slid it across the table under her palm. "Jimmy Tens gave me this yesterday. He ripped the stitches in my bag and sewed a small pocket for me to carry it in." She showed Tao the alteration to her bag for the shiny new switchblade. "He told me he'd show me how to use it and protect myself."

"No complaints here," Tao said. He opened the knife and ran his thumb down the dull side of the blade. He was impressed with the craftsmanship. "Give me a shout if he's outfitting that bag for a handgun, though."

Mute, but with eyes wide, Jayne ran her own thumb pad down

through condensation on her glass.

Tao handed her back the weapon. "You shouldn't be running into much trouble out there. Galen mainly does business with the locals. No passers-through, no one-offs. He pays attention to the word on the street and is careful of who we're dealing with." Tao lifted his bottle to his mouth and emptied it. "If someone is late on payment, we take care of the matter with little fuss. It doesn't happen often."

Jayne sat back as the waitress set another beer on the table. The woman collected the empty and departed.

"Because they're going to want to place another bet or get another loan?" Jayne asked.

Tao leaned forward. He tapped lightly on the tip of her nose with a knuckle. "Got it in one."

≈

Tao held the back door to the bar open for Jayne. She walked in and entered Galen's office toting the paper bag of takeout.

Carol Anne, a tall Italian with large hooped earrings and curly hair hanging to her shoulder blades, stepped to Tao when he entered and ignored Jayne entirely. The woman ran a palm slowly down Tao's chest and pushed her form into his body. "You here to work out the kinks in my neck, T?"

Tao grabbed her hand and placed it down by her side. "Not today."

"Suit yourself," she said, still plastered to his front.

"Carol Anne, this is Michael Ranney's little sister, Jayne," Galen said.

"Hey, kid," the woman said with little warmth.

Tao stepped toward the couch, and Carol Anne leaned her back on the wall by the door. She rested her backside on the back of her folded hands.

Galen set his eyeglasses down on the desk as Jayne slid the bag of food across to him. "*Pontíki mou,* upstairs is a list for DeMoulas so the girls can make some food and stock the refrigerator for the guys. Why don't you grab it and pick up the stuff after school tomorrow?" Galen pulled a slip of paper from the narrow pencil drawer in his desk and made a note. "Give this to Rick in the meat department. We need a lamb on order for Easter on the eighth."

"I thought Easter was in two weeks," Jayne said.

Tao tapped her leg with the tip of his foot from his seat on the couch. "Greek Easter follows the old-timey calendar. Based on the phases of the moon. Galen cooks a whole lamb, head to tail, out in the alley."

Galen leaned back in his chair and pointed at Tao. "Remind Brendan of the date. He did good last year turning the lamb."

Tao smiled. "That's because you had me refilling his beer. He lasted four hours sitting on that milk crate. I wouldn't be surprised if he still had a waffle pattern on his ass."

Galen passed the note to Jayne. He kept his eyes on Tao. "And check with Jimmy that we have enough wire and thread. He needs to sew it up for us on the Saturday."

Carol Anne moved to the desk and perched herself on the corner. She pulled one of the white food cartons from the bag and eyed Jayne out the corner of her eyes. "Off you go, kid. The doors to the apartment are unlocked," she said.

Galen snagged the carton away before Carol Anne could open the top. He gave the woman a harsh glare and turned his attention to Jayne. "You eat yet?"

"Tao bought me dinner. We ate there," Jayne said.

"Good. Call when you're done at DeMoulas tomorrow. We'll swing by and pick you up."

"I will."

Jayne lifted her hand to wave at Tao as she left the office.

Carol Anne moved to the couch. "Speaking of the guys upstairs. You need to get new blood in on the action. Because if it's our same people, and they're dropping their paychecks every week, we're bound to have our own unhappy wives calling downtown. Like they did for the raid over on Broadway. Those sad sacks must've had cops sitting on them for days. You need to tell our guys to bring home flowers every once in a while."

Galen nodded. "I'll have Jimmy stop and talk to everyone to make sure they're keeping up with their responsibilities at home." He slid the pen he was holding behind his ear. "I have a couple calls I can make to get more players. But there's always a risk. With money and booze, there's going to be conflict and a clash of personalities. There haven't been many fights or much trouble with the crew we have now. Not sure I want to upset the applecart."

Tao stretched his arm over the back of the couch behind Carol Anne. "No trouble, except for last month when Tiny threw a footstool through the window on losing that hand with two pairs." He chuckled. "I was tripping over the thing anyways."

"When's the last time you played a hand?" Galen asked.

"I stop up. End of my shift some nights. Just to shoot the shit."

Galen opened a box of lo mein, stabbed it with chopsticks, and pushed it toward Carol Anne. "Take it with you."

She stood, grabbed the carton up briskly with an apparent touch of anger on being dismissed, and exited the office.

Tao sat up and rested his elbows on his knees. "She told me yesterday that the guys are asking if you're going to start up *barbudi* again."

"I held that one night. One night, and there were thirty, forty guys up in that small apartment. Cars all over the street at 3:00 a.m. No. I do that, I need to kick in more to Boston. And if I do it one time, they'll be expecting the cut every month."

"Just asking."

"You remember the ones down on Dutton Street a couple years

ago? Piqued the interest of the boys of the North End. Place was hopping, and our friend doesn't cop on that he needs to be letting the big man win. Or he's just too stubborn to give in. The Italian drops thirty-five large. And I have it on good authority he was talking outside of mowing down everyone in that room that night. Even had the hardware to do the job in his trunk."

"So, no dice."

"No dice," Galen said. He pulled a carton forward to begin his meal. "There's a couple guys out front that might need tending to."

Tao got up and hesitated at the office door. He glanced back. "I had a good talk with the kid today."

Galen curled in two fingers on his hand toward his palm in a sign to speak.

"Jimmy's taken her under his wing," Tao said.

CHAPTER ELEVEN

Over the next few weeks, the weather warmed. Crocuses pushed through the thawing soil, and the streets of Lowell came alive, especially when light of day bled into night. The snows melted to reveal a city landscape ripe for color. And evenings teemed with vehicle and foot traffic.

On a midafternoon, the door opened at the Skillet as Tao made the last entry to the weekly liquor order.

"Incoming," Galen said under his breath from his seat down at the corner of the bar.

Tao slipped the clipboard in his hand down the right side of the cash register. He tucked the pen behind his ear and looked up expectantly. A man stood by the taps, six feet tall, dressed in a tailored two-piece suit, white shirt, and necktie. The interloper jangled a set of keys in his hand and scanned the interior.

Tao stepped up and rested a hand on one of the taps with a look of amusement. "What can I get you?"

"Whiskey neat. And water," the man said.

Tao reached for a lowball glass and looked over to the corner of the bar. Galen nodded his assent, and Tao made a measured pour of amber liquid. He poured water from the tap in a small glass and set both down on the bar. The customer diluted his whiskey a smidgen and took a taste.

The creak of springs on the men's room door had all eyes turning to the back hall. Brendan walked in casually, humming a tune. He made it to a spot on the floor level with Galen's stool and stopped dead in his tracks.

The gentleman before him downed his drink in a blink of an eye and wiped his mouth with the back of his hand before he set after Brendan.

The pint glass Brendan had been cradling to his body slipped from his grasp and shattered on the floor. He turned on his heel and ran back the way he came, missing Jayne by a hair as she exited Galen's office. She pressed tight against the wall and watched Brendan slam his palm on the horizontal release bar of the bar's back door.

Jayne pushed off the wall. She turned toward the front and set her feet shoulders' length apart. Brendan's pursuer slid on leather-soled shoes in a failed effort to stop his momentum. The two collided and came to rest on the floor.

"Geez," Jayne said.

Tao arrived in seconds and helped her stand. Jayne gave him a slight smile when the stranger's attention was drawn to the dirt on his worsted suit coat and pant legs. The man brushed aggressively over the fabric as he stood and ran a sweep of a hand over his hair to cover his bald crown. When he lifted his head, Jayne rubbed at her right knee and glared.

Tao picked Jayne up in his arms with little effort. He walked her over to the bar and set her on a stool beside Galen. "I suggest you leave cash for the whiskey and to compensate the kid," Tao said as the man approached from behind.

The gentleman relented and accepted Tao's sound advice in silence. He pulled his wallet from his coat pocket, placed a few bills down on the bar, and departed. Tao patted Jayne's arm. He slid her the money and made his way back behind the bar. A low whistle came within minutes from the back hall.

"All clear," Galen said.

Brendan walked in with a broom and dustpan from the back closet. He leaned them against the wall and sat on the stool to Jayne's left.

Galen pinched the bridge of his nose between his thumb and middle finger. "If I'm not mistaken, Brendan, that was Judge Brandt from Superior Court. Care to enlighten us on why he's after your hide?"

"The judge is having cash flow issues. Hired me to torch his wife's car."

"What happened?" Galen said.

"I was to take the car down to the railroad trestle, and I had trouble getting her in gear. Lost me head a bit and lit the girl up in the driveway. I'll admit—I was an *edjit*."

Galen and Tao glanced at each other, and their eyes shined with amusement.

Brendan lifted his cap and set it back down more firmly on his head. "What's worse, the key was hidden for me out back the house, and I left it in the ignition. The poor bastard is probably having a time of it explaining himself to the cops and insurance company. Whole dustup's going to tarnish my rep." Brendan stood. He grabbed up the broom and swept the broken glass into a pile. "I'll square it with him tonight, Galen. I didn't want to get into it here."

Jayne hopped off her stool, slipped the cash in her back pocket, and with a nod to Tao headed back to the office. Tao had poked his head in earlier. She had been hard at work finishing up a project for a world history class.

≈

On Thursday, Brendan opened the front door balancing two large coffees and a bag of crullers. He set them down in the middle of the bar, along with the wool cap from his head. He eased onto a stool for a prolonged stay.

"Making amends?" Tao asked. He poured a jigger of bourbon and pulled a pint of beer and slid them over in exchange.

Brendan reached for a napkin and with two shakes of the salt resettled his pint glass. The shot he downed in one and upended on the reservoir.

Tao carried one of the coffees and the bag of donuts to Galen in the corner. He returned to refill a draft for the only other customer at that hour, Sally James. The woman stared at the small, silent black-and-white television in the corner, up over Tao's shoulder. She was sedate, zoning in on the image of an anchor reading the midday news. Sally occasionally worked the corner a few streets over, but she had grown weary of late. And this season, the improving temperature outside was not the draw it had once been.

To keep her sanctuary and avoid a ban by Galen, Sally refrained from soliciting in the bar. Tao made no judgments on how she chose to make her living. He made sure she was not treated with any serious disrespect while in the bar. And he would be forever grateful that prostitution was a vice Galen chose not to manage. Both he and the Greek had seen too many lose their souls to the craft.

"How's it hanging, Brendan?" Tao asked. He turned his attention back to the man and took a sip of the hot, black coffee.

Brendan dropped his hand and pretended to adjust himself. "Bit to the left today. But we'll see with the prevailing winds."

Tao smiled and set to washing glassware in the deep two-well sink. Brendan leaned to the side and pulled a paperback from under Sally's elbow. He held up his hand as she opened her mouth to protest. He turned the book over in his hands. The library catalogue sticker had begun to peel from the bottom of the bind. It was not uncommon for Sally to visit the city library, especially during inclement weather or to hide from whoever was searching for her on the street. She often nursed her drink at the bar and whiled away the hours reading.

"Sherlock Holmes, *The Hound of the Baskervilles*," Brendan said. He lifted his pint glass and swallowed a last mouthful, as if the action was a period in a sentence. "Don't you get frustrated that Doyle never gets to the truth?"

Tao bit as he wiped his hands with a towel. "What truth?"

"Most people miss it—being ignorant pieces of worthless space. Present company excluded, of course." Head straight, Brendan shifted his eyes to Sally and shrugged.

"Hey!" she said. She grabbed the book and tucked it back under her arm.

Brendan smiled and pushed his glass toward Tao. "Just messing with you, girl." Brendan sprinkled a shake of salt on a new napkin. "As I was saying … people fail to grasp the obvious. The man was a psychotic, paranoid, homicidal maniac."

Tao filled a new pint glass and pushed the tap closed with the heel of his hand. He set down Brendan's drink. "Doyle or Holmes? You understand he's only a character in a book, right?"

"That's what they want you to believe," Brendan said.

"Who's they?" Sally asked.

Brendan continued, neglecting to answer the question. "You ever wonder how he solved all those cases? Pulled all those minuscule, crucial clues out of his ass?"

"Go on," Tao said.

"It was all him. Sherlock Holmes. Did his coke, played his violin, learned carnal knowledge of his buddy Watson there. And set up each and every crime he investigated."

"What?" Tao said.

Brendan reached in his right-hand pocket for his pack of cigarettes. "And. The most obvious of all." He lifted his gaze back to Tao. "Your man was Moriarty. The whole time."

"Bullshit," Tao said.

Brendan sat back on his stool with a smile and a nod, obviously proud of his means of deduction. Sally stared at Brendan with eyes wide and lips parted as Tao wiped the bar distractedly with a towel and shook his head in wonder.

Sally swung her stool to the side by bracing the ball of one foot on the bar rail. "You're in serious need of a ride on the blue bus to Danvers State, man," she said.

Brendan laughed. "The looney bin? Honey, they don't pick you up in no blue bus to that hell. They pick you up in some nondescript panel van."

Sally and Tao exchanged a look that brought a smile to Brendan's eyes before he continued. "Just saying. You get a lift to a place like that, they're going to keep you in the dark as long as humanly possible. To get your ass inside and situated."

Sally nodded. "I had an uncle up there at one time. My dad used to threaten to drop my little brother off for a stay."

"Cool-looking place," Tao said.

"Cool, as in scary as *shite*," Brendan said. "If memory serves, those Gothic buildings on the hill were the spot of the very first frontal lobotomies. These days there's also no hesitation on plugging people into light sockets either."

Galen ended a phone conversation at the end of the bar with his voice raised a notch. He set down the receiver.

Tao lifted his chin once to Galen and gestured toward Brendan with his head. "Should have caught the discussion last week, boss. Our man here believes cul-de-sacs exist because we, as a species, refuse to face our mortality."

Excited, Brendan stood and leaned in to see the corner, past Sally. "It's true. They're turning up everywhere now. All those new developments on the Tewksbury line? All on cul-de-sacs. What is so wrong with a dead end?"

"Ever think it might be in some building code?" Tao said.

"Building code or not, no way in hell I'm buying a house on Denial Road, Tao."

Tao opened a new box of bar napkins. "For when you move out of that trailer of yours?"

"Mansions on lollipop lanes. The rich pricks."

"Cool your jets, man," Tao said.

"Go ahead. Set up house on Nine Stages of Hell Circle. See where that gets you."

Galen smiled and dropped his head to read the headlines of the day.

Brendan settled back on his stool and rested his left arm on the bar. "Hey, Galen, care to buy some raffle tickets? Support a worthy cause?"

"What is it?" Galen asked.

"Galway Roads and Bridges Fund. Most are still getting around on dirt roads back home."

"And the bridges part?"

"They're planning to construct a bridge on the far side of Galway City."

Tao opened a new bottle of ouzo and screwed in a spout. "Into the ocean?"

"This money going to buy guns, Brendan?" Galen tugged on the small curls of hair at the back of his head.

"It's a donation for the betterment of the infrastructure on the west coast of Ireland. Plain and simple." Brendan shrugged his shoulders high and stared down into his beer. "Not saying my brethren don't deserve a hand up in the Troubles."

"Give me two books," Galen said.

"I haven't said how much."

Galen set down his paper and looked at Brendan intently. "Two books. And let me know if there are any you can't sell at the end."

Brendan nodded solemnly.

Tao witnessed the immediate change in the man's demeanor and a settling of his body on the stool. It was evident that the relentless news of escalating violence out of Ireland weighed heavy on Brendan's psyche, even though it had been years since he emigrated to America. It had only been in January that the British Army serving in Northern Ireland were given authorization to use machine guns against men and women they deemed to be a threat. That was coupled with a shoot-without-warning directive.

In the quiet that descended in the bar, Sally recommenced staring at the television program. Galen answered another series of phone calls. He doodled and recorded marks in a small notebook by his right hand. And Brendan McHugh drank without uttering a single word for the next hour. The man slipped out the front door and Tao added his libations to a tab, a tally that was to be squared at week's end.

Tao pointed to the Sherlock Holmes tale under Sally's elbow. "Can I read that when you're done?"

CHAPTER TWELVE

The mid-century brick building sat on a corner that offered minimal parking. The structure had tall windows shrouded in heavy drapes for privacy. A small sign, hand-carved and low to the ground, was staked at the head of the property. The single bulb of a covered lamp hung over a proper door, and a steep staircase led to an entrance on the second floor.

The private club's membership was in flux. It held a roster of old-timers deep-rooted in the status quo and young men settling down after coming of age in the sixties in an ephemeral mist of antiestablishment sentiment. Recent members were recruited from men returning from Vietnam and men raising families and anchoring themselves in neighborhoods while attending a church regularly and joining one of the many social organizations in the city. The club provided a blanket of communal protection, whether real or perceived, and entrance was selective.

Jayne Ranney turned the mechanical twist doorbell twice and stepped back to the rail to allow clearance as the door swung wide. She smiled a greeting to the day manager. She stepped in and handed him two white envelopes and a short stack of football cards. She walked over maroon carpet to the back corner, passing a bar framed in hardwood. She made her way down a narrow set of stairs and entered a cramped room of damaged barstools, cases of liquor stock, and pallets, on which stood four kegs of beer. A group of men sat on blue metal chairs in the corner. They played hearts on a scarred and littered card table as a dissipating gray cloud of stale cigar smoke hovered in the air.

Harold Fuller looked up. He was around sixty, dressed in plaid polyester pants that rested high on his waist. His hair was slick with Grecian Formula. He set down his cards on the table and sat back. He tipped up on two legs of his chair. "Hey, sweetie. Galen give you the line on Miami tonight?"

"They're giving six," Jayne said. She shrugged her book bag from her shoulder and pulled a small package free. She unwrapped newspaper from a clear bottle of *tsipouro* and leaned over the table to set it down beside Mr. Fuller.

A man on Jayne's right reached a long arm around her waist and pulled down hard on her hip. He sat her forcefully on the edge of his thigh.

"Let me up," Jayne said. She dropped her bag to the floor and used the table to pull herself up and away from the man's grasp.

He was younger than the others and wore the uniform pants, shirt, and tie of a delivery man. The jacket on the chair had the stitching of a name. But the tag was turned inward just enough to be indecipherable.

"You don't want to sit on my lap? Give me some luck on this next hand?" he said.

"No. And don't touch me."

The man stood, and the expression of amusement he had worn since she crossed the room dropped from his face like overhead shutters being pulled down at closing time outside a shop.

Jayne bent to retrieve her bag.

The man stepped forward and grabbed her above her elbow, pulling her so her back was to his front. He stooped down and snaked his arm around her body, up under her shirt, and let his open palm lie on the soft, warm skin of her belly. "Nice," he said.

Mr. Fuller leaned forward and adjusted himself on the chair in obvious discomfort at the sight. "You got a death wish, son? The girl there works for the Greek."

Her assailant slowly moved his hand over her left ribcage. He breathed in deep as he pulled her in closer to his body. "She's no tattle-tale," he said.

For Jayne, the move hit a raw nerve. She set her right foot back between the man's legs and leaned her dead weight into him and to the side. The shift worked to set the bastard off balance instantly. As he moved to catch himself, she stepped out. She turned and swung her bag up by its strap, up with force, and into the man's nose.

He cried out and brought up two hands to stem the flow of blood. Jayne took two steps back for distance. She dropped her bag and in a fluid motion swung her leg forward and up with feeling directly into the distracted man's crotch.

He dropped to the floor as he appeared to fail to catch a breath. He finally let out a low groan in protest, his hands having left his face to nurse the more recent injury. Mr. Fuller and the others had stood from their chairs and looked on in wonder. Jayne hiked her bag over her shoulder and made her way past a body that rolled slowly from side to side. She stepped over it without a glance down at her accomplishment. She continued across the room and ascended the stairs. And as she hit the street, the adrenaline in her system carried her in a hurried state to the bar.

≈

Jayne stood across from Galen as he sat at his desk. She pulled a metal cash-box from her bag and set it down with care as she waited for her boss to end a phone conversation.

He hung up and adjusted his glasses. "What's this?"

"The take on the action from last night at the Golden Gloves."

"They could have just given you the cash instead of you lugging this heavy thing around all afternoon."

She patted the top of the box. "It was nothing," she said.

Galen saw a tremor in her hand and leaned forward. He grabbed her wrist gently before Jayne could step away. "What's wrong? Something happen today?"

Tao took that moment to walk in the open door to the office with Jimmy Tens in tow. Their eyes were on Jayne and stayed there as Tao addressed Galen. "Harry over at the club called out front. Took me a while to understand him. Thought he was dying. Turns out he was laughing his ass off."

Galen let go of Jayne's wrist and leaned back in his chair as Jimmy stepped closer to the desk by his side.

Tao lifted his chin at Jayne. "Our little one here kicked his nephew Kevin's balls so hard up into the back of his throat, it'll be days before they descend. May have broke the weasel's nose to boot."

"What happened?" Galen asked Jayne.

"Kevin put his hands on her. According to Harry," Tao said as he crossed his arms over his chest.

Galen moved the metal cashbox to the side. "That true?"

Jayne nodded.

Galen laid his palm on his shirt pocket, and his fingers slightly gripped the material. "You all right?"

She lifted her shoulders but didn't let them fall immediately. "I hit him before he could do anything to me. I couldn't reach my knife, so I broke his hold the way Jimmy showed me. It was easy from there. Jimmy's been showing me stuff. I wasn't sure I'd remember what he told me if something happened. But it was right there."

Galen nodded. "You're going to keep up those lessons," he said. He looked over at Jimmy and back to Jayne. "Why don't you go out front with Tao. I'll finish up here and take you down to the Rex for some dinner."

Jayne relaxed, and some of the tension left her body. She stepped to the office door and felt Tao's hand on her shoulder as they made their way out to the bar.

≈

Jimmy moved to the front of the desk. He had grown his beard quite long over the past few months, and the monastic look only added to the menace in his eyes. "How much can I hurt him?"

Galen looked up as he felt a small smile play on his lips. "I'm surprised you asked." He sat back in his chair and rocked it on its springs. "First, have Bill pull Kevin's membership. And if Harry defends that nephew of his, have Bill pull Harry's as well. I don't want Jayne having any problems over there. Make that clear. And get the full story."

Jimmy reached into the front pocket of his jeans and pulled out his keys.

Galen stopped rocking and sat forward, setting his forearms on the desk. "You can hurt him. But like Tao says, don't go puncturing a lung. And no permanent marks. Bearing those two conditions—have at him."

Jimmy left the office and went out the door to the back alley. Galen lifted the cashbox in front of him and pulled off a small key taped to the underside. He made a mental note to stop at Komidís for a paper on the way to the restaurant with Jayne. News from Greece always proved to be a good distraction from his thoughts.

≈

At the end of the week, and at the end of a run, Jayne walked through the back door of the Skillet. She unbuttoned her jacket as she entered Galen's office. Tao stood leaning with his shoulder against the far wall as the two men wrapped up a discussion. They appeared to be squaring away a dis-

89

agreement with the liquor distributor, who was attempting to push a low-grade vodka on the bar. Jayne sat on the couch and fiddled with a loose thread on the pocket of her jacket.

"Here she is," Galen said. He turned his attention to Jayne and slowly shook his head. "Jayne. There any reason Jacob Collier's calling, asking me to add milk to his buy tomorrow?"

Jayne tugged once at the hem of her shirt and sat up straighter from a slouch.

Galen lowered his glasses with a finger hooked in the bridge. "You're dropping twenty Valium. So, not only are you supplying a narcotic to Mr. Collier on my behalf, you're performing a community service as well?"

Tao excused himself and with a light pat on Jayne's head left the office to return to the bar.

Jayne pulled the satchel from her bag and stood to set it on Galen's desk. She met his eyes. "You have to see him, Galen. See his house. I don't think the guy leaves it. Ever. He told me his brother drops by, maybe once a month, if that. There are stacks of books and coffee cans in the hallway. Glass bottles and parts to a car when there are no cars in his driveway. There's barely room to walk in the house. He tells me he has a couple cats. I haven't seen one yet."

"I know his situation, Jayne. If you're worried about Jacob, or anyone else for that matter, come talk to me."

Jayne sat back down on the edge of the couch cushion.

Galen leaned back in his chair. "What are you doing up in his house? You can do business right inside the door, then be on your way. Didn't Tao teach you to make the stops quick? Not to expose yourself."

She nodded.

"After the club business, you have me worried," Galen said.

"Jesus Christ. You can't think that was my fault."

Galen frowned. "Jayne, I don't mind you swearing, but don't take the Lord's name in vain in front of me again."

She worried her hands on her lap.

Galen sat forward once again. "I didn't say you were to blame. I just need to know you're being careful. Last Tuesday and Wednesday, on your runs, you didn't call in once."

"I didn't have any problems."

"Yes, but you started your route straight from school without stopping in first. How could we be sure you were squared away? Days you start your run at the bell, call the bar at the first pay phone. Give us the chance to change up your route. Let us know you're okay."

"I'll call. I promise."

"Good. Now go home—get some rest. And tomorrow, I don't need you back in here until late morning." Galen emptied the satchel onto his desk as she left the office. He counted out a sum of cash she had collected from the fire captain east of the city center. He secured the lot in the safe and rubbed his forehead as the seeds of a headache took hold.

He ticked off what he knew of Jacob Collier. Nothing in the man's character made him any threat to his girl. Jacob lived alone in the house of his birth. He lived off an inheritance he shared with his brother, who served in Korea and returned to take up with a wife and three children in Arlington. Jacob invested some of the money in properties downtown and collected monthly rents. He paid a fee to a property management company to suit his needs with the rentals. He had dated a woman back in the day, but it never amounted to a lasting relationship, likely due to his isolation and proclivity to collect things. A compulsion passed down from his mother.

For Mrs. Collier it had been newspapers, stacked high in rooms, hallways, and a good portion of the attic. Maybe, in her encapsulated world, she strived to harbor and harness history. History she could touch by picking up one of the newspapers from her collection and physically holding it.

On her passing and out of respect, Jacob cleared the home of the stacks of paper. The act may well have saved the property from fire. But the house was still packed to the rafters. It held books, dishware, and appliances. Of turntables alone, Galen counted a Victrola, a Thorens, and three others in various stages of disassembly. Jacob kept them all, even when they were no longer of use.

And after burying both parents in a six-month span and the assassination of John F. Kennedy on a Friday, November 22, 1962, Jacob refused to venture out of the house and off the property. He spoke of sadness that his mother had missed out on the headline of the ages. And he relayed his fears that the streets had, on that fateful day, descended into chaos. As if before that moment in time, sunflowers sprang from the border of sidewalks of an idealistic society, not the refuse and broken glass of today. As if the country, his community, and his surroundings were not as they once had been.

Galen never held such an idealistic view of his adopted homeland. He was deep-rooted in practical beliefs. And they served him well. He rubbed his forehead once again and made his way out to the bar. He signaled to Tao for ouzo and leaned an elbow down. Tao reached for the bottle and set down a glass before him. Galen pulled a short stack of twenties from his wallet and placed them on the rail. He slid the bills forward as Tao poured his drink.

"Have Jimmy take your truck over to Jacob's house. See what's what and stock his fridge. Get the man cleaned up," Galen said.

"Why does Jimmy need my truck?"

"Jayne says the house is in a bad state again. Get Jimmy to pick up a couple of the guys if he needs help. Give them the extra cash to get some of it cleared out."

"I don't know. Jacob gets testy about people messing with his things."

Galen shrugged. "It's worth a go. Have Jimmy stop back and see me afterward. Let me know how he made out."

Tao ran a thumb down across his facial scar. "Our little mouse getting to you, boss?"

Galen upended the shot of ouzo and, with a groan, set down the glass. "*Stamáta.*"

≈

Summer arrived, and Jayne and her classmates were let out from school. Her schedule working for Galen remained the same, but she found she spent less and less time at home, whether it was dinner down at the bar, sharing plates of souvlaki from the Olympia Restaurant and overloading her belly on red-sauced potatoes, or sharing pizza with Jimmy and Tao as the Red Sox played a game on the television.

Watching baseball with them reminded Jayne of a Celtics playoff game mid-April, a school night. The sound on the television was off as they watched the game in the apartment above the bar. Tao tuned a radio to a play-by-play announcer, Johnny Most. He had a harsh, raspy voice that filled the room with energy and excitement. It was Tao's night off, and he had invited two of his friends from the neighborhood. Jimmy sat beside her on the couch, exhibiting a rare enthusiasm, jumping up and gesturing toward the television on calls by the officials, swearing and celebrating as the game progressed. Boston beat New York, and Jimmy walked her home after with a bounce in his step.

At least once a week over the summer, when the weather was right, a barbecue grill in the back alley was put to use. They cooked up cheese-burgers and *loukániko*, pork chops, and ears of corn still nestled in their husks. And everyone ate. Brendan McHugh, Sally James, and whoever else happened to stop in on a sunny afternoon. Jayne sat at a picnic table that had been dragged into the alley and listened to the banter. Mainly Brendan talking Jimmy's ear off and Jimmy ignoring the Irishman, only speaking to make a request for oregano or the bottle of red wine vinegar from the upstairs kitchen.

Jimmy brought her to the movies on two nights in July, first to see *Marlowe*, a detective story, then to *The Way of the Dragon*. Jayne was mesmerized by the fighting moves of the star, Bruce Lee, on the big screen.

She connected with Émile and a small group of friends some mornings. They rode their bicycles, sat on the grasses of the Common, and watched pickup games of basketball. Émile joined in and glanced back at her after each good play he managed. He paid her attention and rode behind her on his bicycle—out a bit to the right, protecting her from the cars on the road. She cut out on her friends early in the day, headed to Galen's office before her runs, and often sat at the bar for a glass bottle of Coke in the afternoons.

In August, Jayne was able to coax Jacob Collier out to his back porch for hands of gin rummy. They looked out over the yard, over the grass and weeds that had grown to their natural height, nearly hiding a rundown shed. The brush and bushes in the yard contained hordes of birds that fluttered in and out of cover, but their song was silent in afternoon heat. She considered asking Galen to send someone to mow the lawn and trim the plants. But the tangled, impassible condition of the space would take fire to burn it back enough to be workable. She was proud of getting Jacob out into the fresh air and stopped by every few days.

Soon, school started and Jayne's junior year had begun.

CHAPTER THIRTEEN

Byrd White stood in the doorway of a room at the Billerica House of Correction. He was dressed in civilian clothes and had his hands in the front pockets of his slacks. Michael Ranney walked through the large, peripherally lit visitors' section of the prison with a guard in tow. He entered the room, slipping past Byrd into a space not much larger than two cells, set side to side.

Byrd and Michael refrained from greeting each other until the door to the room closed. Michael took a seat at the table in one of the two chairs.

Byrd lifted a hand and scrubbed at the short hair on the crown of his head. "Putting aside that it's the middle of the night, that you have the guard out there wrapped around your finger tight enough that this meeting is happening, and you somehow pulled my unlisted home number out of your ass—how the hell did you know I wasn't on shift tonight?"

Michael looked over his shoulder and turned his chair to face away from the small square window in the door.

Byrd stepped over and leaned his back on the wall.

"I didn't know you were home," Michael said. "I called your house the last three nights. Knew you'd get a night off at some point. And the screw? I told him you're on the job and promised him a nice fresh box of Cuban cigars."

"You want to explain the cloak-and-dagger routine? Anything to get me off asking about the logistics of you getting such a rare commodity up in here."

Michael was quiet a moment, and Byrd felt a shift in the air. A sense that picking up the phone earlier may have been a mistake.

"Tell me about Sergeant Hamel," Michael said. He pulled out a pack of cigarettes and matches from his pocket and lit up.

Byrd stepped to the table and put two hands on the back of the spare chair. "You got me over here about Ray Hamel? A guy who's been dead nearly a year?"

"I need you to tell me if there was an investigation into his demise."

"Ray was out on disability, in pain, drinking too much gin, and ate his gun. What's there to investigate?"

"Did they do an autopsy?"

"I'm sure. But the back of the man's head was splattered like a Rorschach test on his kitchen wall. I can't see that the ME had too much trouble with his findings."

Michael curled in the rest of his fingers on the hand holding his cigarette and looked at the dirt under his fingernails. "Could there be someone who looked into his death, under the radar? Have you heard talk?"

"No. It was suicide by service revolver. Black-and-white, cut-and-dried, if you get my drift. Or did you drag me down here to tell me different?"

"What about at the wake or funeral?"

"What about them?"

"What was your sense of things?"

"Not to speak ill of the dead, but Ray was not a well-liked man. But he was still a brother officer. And they turned up in droves. The department, as well as police and fire from bordering towns. Too many for me to be honing in on some backroom conversation."

Michael rubbed smoke out of his eye and stared down at the table. "Were you at his house after he was found? Anything strike you?"

"The call went out, and anyone in hearing distance booked it to the house. Whole department walked through that kitchen at some point.

Both before and after he was bagged and tagged."

"Who found him?"

"His daughter. Swung by the house after dropping her kids at school." Byrd pulled out the chair and sat down. "Want to tell me why I'm here, Michael? What do you have for me?"

"I need a friend."

Byrd sat and waited.

"I feel like I'm being watched in here," Michael said.

Byrd let out a chuckle. "You're kidding me, right?"

"I have good instincts, and they're talking to me. Setting me on edge."

"I don't know how much assistance I can give. I'm pretty low on the totem pole in the department. A department that has no jurisdiction on you here. I'm not going to reach out and talk to the warden to say you feel on edge. Unless you tell me you're in immediate danger. You in fear for your life, Michael?"

"No. Just need you to call me if you hear anything on Ray Hamel. Or if you can dig anything up. That's all."

"You drag me out of bed and tease me as if you're wielding an opener for a big can of worms. And leave me with nothing."

"Chalk up the visit to a heads-up. A warning. Even on the outside, man, the danger comes from guys operating in your own backyard. In plain sight."

Byrd shook his head in frustration as he walked to the door and knocked twice. "Now you're speaking in riddles. Make sure you have something useful to tell me next time you pull me in here."

Michael stubbed out his smoke in the small ashtray sunk into the edge of the table. He appeared happy to hear Byrd was open to further discussion on the subject.

≈

On his return home, Byrd puttered around before he was able to drop back into a restless slumber that was broken after four short hours. He came awake with a start and sat up on his couch. The quick movement caused a flash of pain to stab down through his lower back. He groaned and rested his elbows on his knees. He covered his face with his hands and breathed in through his teeth, his jaw shut tight.

A nightmare, one that left him with an overwhelming feeling of helplessness, had again eaten up precious rest as snapshots of a scene of past horror flashed through his mind. The memory was from when he was portable, still walking the beat. Byrd picked up a detail shift on a construction site on Riverside Street. It began as a routine gig as he facilitated the flow of traffic around the busy area. Byrd was unaware that a truck was moving a large fuel tank that day. The skin of the tank had ruptured, and propane was leaking and spreading silently over the roadway like an invisible, combustible blanket. And on a spark, it ignited, the fuel lighting up a row of cars, one by one in a steady succession.

Byrd sprang into action alongside civilians. The brave who rushed to free men, women, and children from cages of flame. The sight, sounds, and smells were imprinted on Byrd's memory. Visited with near total recall. In sleep, a harmless journey could lead him back to that road, back to that day and a series of still images that trapped him until he broke free from the replay in his mind.

All in all, shifts on night patrol had been routine the last year. They were shifts Byrd drove alone. In contrast, walking routes by the LPD were manned by two men, a rule strictly enforced after the assault on John Winn, an officer set upon while checking that the doors of a church were secure.

Officers on foot called in regularly using one of the many hard-wired call boxes in the city. These days, Byrd used a radio in his cruiser to contact the station. He followed a route he changed up every third day, passing by neighborhoods prone to late-night activity and parking behind businesses and properties that butted up against the railway tracks to Boston or wooded expanses. He also pulled over motorists, issued citations, and performed field sobriety tests. He called into the station and was dispatched to family disputes. He followed up on reports of breaking and entering. He broke up bar brawls.

Byrd's goal was to defuse situations, separate battling spouses, record instances of robbery, and impart assurances of the department's ability to investigate damages to person or property. He took people too inebriated or drugged up to function into protective custody. And at the end of a shift, he returned to the station, parked his cruiser, and wrote up his reports.

On choosing the profession, Byrd was aware of the inherent danger. He learned over time that there were moments he would be tested to stand tall. Days he felt proud, proud that the work he was doing was reflecting positively on his community. But he also struggled silently with police culture, the tendency for his brothers to view violence in the home as a private matter and turn a blind eye. An acceptance of the practice of showing preferential treatment to people that had even a sliver of influence in the department. An oath among the men to hold true a loyalty and trust among themselves that would never be broken or questioned, even under the most egregious of circumstances.

But Byrd chose to work within those confines. As long as he gave it his best, he was satisfied. He stood from his couch and stretched as early-morning light warmed a stripe over his foot. The sound of a garbage truck that rumbled past on the street below seeped into the apartment. He thought back over his visit to Billerica. Thought about the nagging, bothersome kernel of intrigue planted in his brain by Michael Ranney, ward of the State of Massachusetts.

Byrd had tertiary access to investigations within the department, but he was not confident he would be able to ascertain if there had been any doubt in the cause of death of Ray Hamel. He heard no question about the obvious means of suicide. To dispel the unrelenting thoughts in his head, though, he showered and dressed while deciding on a plan of action.

≈

Byrd pulled his personal vehicle, a Ford Galaxie Fastback, up the driveway of a small, single-family house in Pawtucketville. The grass in the yard was high, and a mower, with its engine exposed to the elements, sat beside the garage. A buzzing hum of insects surrounded Byrd as he approached the home. He stepped up on the small porch and knocked on the front door. He had learned by making a phone call that Cecilia Hamel, Ray's daughter, had taken up residence in the home.

Byrd had dated Cecilia in high school, but it was a short-lived relationship. He remembered her as having a brash personality. Brash in the assertive sense, not rude. She tended to be loud, with the skills of a witty debater. She had won arguments regardless of the strength in her belief in her own stance. He could have used her over the years in a few rounds with his family and friends.

The door opened wide, and Cecilia greeted Byrd with a hesitant smile. The colorful peasant shirt she wore struck Byrd as surprisingly feminine for a woman who stood at his height, with broad shoulders and curly hair fashioned tight to her head.

"Hey," he said.

"What you doing here, Byrd?"

"I'm here about Ray."

Cecilia lost the smile. "To pay your respects? After all this time?" she asked. She held her youngest back with a hand to the small, curious child's chest. "Because I saw you at the funeral, and I think we're all paid up here."

"No, Cecilia. Sorry. Ray was a mentor of mine, and I wonder if you could give me a few minutes."

"Mentor? Now that's some bullshit."

Byrd winced at his misstep as she shooed the child up the stairs. "Ceci..."

"Dad was an asshole. Doesn't mean I didn't love him. But no one, and I mean no one, thought of him as a mentor. Hell, he and his buddies got their kicks out of hazing all the up-and-coming recruits in the department. Are you telling me you weren't subjected to that shit too?"

"Some."

"So, stop pulling my leg."

"I'll get right to it, then." He slipped his hands into his pants pockets. "I want a look at his room. Just a few minutes, and I'll be gone."

Cecilia sighed, backed up, and made room for Byrd to enter.

"Thanks. I truly am sorry for your loss." Byrd followed her down a short hall and out through the kitchen.

She opened a door to the garage and motioned for him to enter ahead of her. She went down a step and pointed to three boxes stacked in the corner. "Those are his things. That's what's left of Dad's personal belongings. Doesn't look like much, does it?"

Byrd walked over and lifted the cover off the top box. Cecilia stepped down and leaned a hip on the Chevy parked in the bay.

"We used to do takeout every Friday. I'd bring the kids by and do his laundry. Clean up the place. I always thought it was a hassle. It never occurred to me that it was the highlight of my week. That I looked forward to pizza and toasted subs with my dad. I hate Fridays now."

Byrd looked over with sympathy in his eyes. "Did you know he was depressed?"

She shrugged. "He seemed the same old guy. Griping about whatever was bothering him. Taxes, inflation, you name it. He didn't talk about his feelings, none of us do. Ever hear any of the guys at the station admit they were depressed?"

He shook his head and smiled. "Never."

"Didn't think so."

"Your mother come up for the funeral? I don't remember seeing her there."

"No. She hasn't been back since she left us fifteen years ago. Married another cop, if you can believe it."

He lifted out a small bowling trophy from the box and tilted it to read the inscription. "Can I go through these? I can be out of your hair in ten, fifteen minutes."

"Take your time, Byrd. I need to give the kids a bath. There's beer in the refrigerator, if it's not too early for you."

"Thanks. And I don't mean to be crass, Ceci, but did you happen to keep aside anything to remember him by? I was just wondering, since he didn't leave a note, if maybe you have something that might help explain what was going on in his head."

Cecilia scowled. "Nothing. I dumped his clothes to Goodwill and cleaned out his closet so I could give my kids the bedroom. I gave his bowling ball and his team shirt to a buddy of his, and everything else was junked. Except what's in those boxes. You want to stay and explain to me what this is all about? Don't you think I deserve to know why you're here poking around?"

"It could be nothing. But I promise, if I find anything that will help, I'll let you know."

"That's not the same thing as telling me the truth, now, is it?" she said as she headed back into the kitchen.

Byrd spread out the items in the boxes on the hood of the car and on an old weight bench that was covered in a fine layer of dust. He mentally inventoried two stale cigars in their wrappers, a pair of gloves, letters from Ray's ex-wife tied in a piece of twine, likely from when they were courting, a photo of Ray and his coworkers smiling and raising their glasses in a bar downtown, more bowling trophies, a faded sweatshirt from his days as a college student, papers and trinkets people generally stowed in their sock drawer, and a framed photo of Ray on the day he was sworn in as a patrolman, his proud mother by his side. He was curious why Cecilia chose not to keep the photographs to display up on the mantel, or at least in a drawer for safekeeping.

Byrd found nothing of significance to suit his needs. No clue to Ray's state of mind or any recent keepsakes. He stepped to the side of the car and peered in a window before trying the door. He had seen Ray park the car on a number of occasions at work. He slid into the driver's seat and turned his head to the back seat, which was littered with Cheerios and cracker crumbs. A couple small, green plastic soldiers lay amid the debris. The car was obviously still in use.

He checked the ashtrays and pulled down the visors, causing a pen to drop in his lap. He leaned over, popped the button on the glove compartment, and found a small notebook, the type he himself carried on the job. Byrd's reports were written up after each shift ended. Without the notes he took meticulously, he would be hard-pressed to provide wholly accurate information.

He sat back in the seat and flipped a few pages to find an obvious record of surveillance—lines of dates and times, locations. One initial, the letter "C" written to designate the subject, and short notes set up as questions and answers arrived at, as if Ray was carrying on a discussion of one. He turned over the book and found "7L3" etched in the back cover. The numbers and letter were traced over so many times, they were embedded in the cardboard backing. If it was a license plate, being only three digits, it belonged to someone with connections. He would run it as soon as he reached work.

Byrd got out of the car and put the notepad in his pocket. He delivered the items back into their respective boxes and quietly let himself out through the door on the side of the garage. He would thank Cecilia if he had reason to see her again. She did not need to know about the notes Ray kept. To Byrd, they were work product, even if the dates written were during Ray's medical leave.

≈

"7L3" was indeed a license plate. A government-issued license plate belonging to the Boston Division of the Federal Bureau of Investigation. The vehicle of record was a black 1970 Plymouth Fury with no markings. It was assigned to Agent Thomas Archibald Curry.

Byrd stared for an inordinate amount of time at the car as it sat parked in a spot designated for the deputy superintendent. Byrd put his cruiser in drive and made his way over to Broadway and one of the Greek coffee shops, one that was cover for a small backroom gambling den. Byrd pulled over on a side street next to the canal and motioned for a teenage boy who was standing in the doorway smoking a cigarette. The boy rapped his fingers on the closed door behind him with his arm straight down at his side as if to conceal the signal. He walked over slowly to Byrd's window.

Byrd leaned his arm on the car door, his elbow jutting out the window. "No trouble, kid. Can you go roust Manny and have him come outside?" he asked.

"I don't know no Manny."

"Either you get him, or I get out and find him myself."

The boy turned and skipped back over to the shop. He entered, and in under two minutes, Manny Laczkó slid into the back seat of the cruiser.

He met Byrd's eyes in the rearview mirror. "Pull farther down the street."

Laczkó was one of five who worked vice in the department. He wore street clothes, and if asked by another officer, he would insist he was undercover. But few of the players on the streets were unaware he was on the job, and none in the coffee shop.

Byrd moved the car. He set it in park and turned in his seat, draping an arm casually around the headrest. "What can you tell me about the fed who's taken up shop at the station?"

Manny shrugged. He glanced out the side window and turned his head back to Byrd. "He's been on a couple ride-alongs, during busts. Mostly he's going through records, though. Documenting stats and procedure. Personally, I think it chaps his ass that he hasn't been designated a 'special agent' with the bureau. He's a prick. Doesn't speak to anyone under rank of lieutenant unless absolutely necessary."

"What's he doing here?"

"Observing, picking up wisdom for some centralized bureau for drugs that Nixon wants to set up. I don't know how that's supposed to work, if you ask me. The fight's local. Anyone can see that. On the streets. Not down in Washington in some office with the suits."

"Anything strike you, other than him being a prick?"

"Haven't had any real discussion with the guy to know anything. What's the deal?"

"Curious, I guess."

"The guy's not long for the city. Rumor has it whatever scouting he's doing is coming to an end. Something about field guys being recalled soon." Manny pointed with a thumb up the street. "I need to get back to what I need to get back to."

"Thanks, Manny," Byrd said.

Manny got out of the car and approached the shop. He swung his arm around the young boy's shoulders and walked with him through the front door.

≈

Byrd reached out to Michael Ranney this time. He decided not to chance visiting the jail during the day and drawing attention to himself. Nor would he hold out until his next shift off. He sat back in one of the chairs in the now-familiar room, in full uniform sans the sidearm. He listened as footfalls approached the door.

Michael walked in and smiled. "This an official visit?"

Byrd watched and waited for the door to close behind Michael. "Yes and no. Because, to protect myself, I really should start documenting these visits. But for now, we're off the books."

Michael took the remaining chair and glanced up at the window.

Byrd released one of the buttons of his uniform to ease the tension in his shoulder. "What is it you dropped in my lap here, Michael? Because I need answers now."

"You find out anything for me?"

"I need you to be straight with me."

"I will. You first." Michael shook out a cigarette from his pack and lit up.

Byrd sat back and placed the open palms of his hands on the table. "The documentation on Ray Hamel's suicide is in order. I even spoke with the recording officer. No surprises. I haven't heard or seen any other query into the matter. That being said—a couple days ago, I took initiative and retraced steps at the Hamel home. Almost all memory of him has been shuffled out to the garage. His daughter, who's taken up residency of the property, offered up no theory on Ray checking out. Which leaves the act up to means—a service revolver and opportunity—Ray lived alone, and the decision may have been spur-of-the-moment. A moment of weakness he could never come back from."

Michael blew smoke toward the ceiling. He glanced again at the little window in the door. "So, nothing. You found nothing."

"What I found were notes Ray made while on medical leave. Notes he made while tracking someone. The dates prove it was weeks of surveillance."

"Of who?"

"Agent Thomas Curry. Ray Hamel was casing an FBI agent out of Boston without being made, as far as I can gather. I never knew Ray had it in him. The last entry was dated the day before he checked out."

"What was the entry?"

"Chadwick. Then blank pages. Now, you going to start talking to me?"

Michael extinguished his cigarette, stood up, and walked over to lean on the wall beside the door. He hesitated, as if needing time to reach a decision. He brought his head up and looked Byrd in the eyes. "The fed. I watched him kill Hamel."

Byrd let out a long breath. "Talk."

"I was out at the Chadwick School. Thought I was alone. Middle of the night."

"A building that's been shuttered."

"I was scoping out some piping."

"Pulling copper."

"Anyway. I stumbled on the two of them talking. This guy Curry. Dressed like Inspector Erskine, now that you mention it. He put a choke hold on Hamel. And, well—lights out."

"What were they saying to each other."

"The fed was crooked as a dog's hind leg. Your man caught on and wanted a piece. I read in the paper later about that drug rehab program. SHARE. Curry was, or is, stealing from the program."

"That's a bit far-fetched. This fed sits down to dinner with the deputy superintendent. My captain. I mean, why risk a career?"

Michael shrugged. "Who's going to question what an FBI agent is doing in an official capacity? Honestly, you catch sight of the guy? He probably considers Lowell out in the boondocks."

Byrd fidgeted in his seat. "How'd you know Ray was dead? Could he have been still alive?"

"G-man rolled the old buck up in a tarp and dropped him in his trunk."

"Then what?"

"Then he drives away before the sun comes up, and I hightail it out of there."

"What aren't you telling me? Why get me involved? I've been told he's leaving the area soon. Back to Washington."

Michael pushed off the wall and crossed his arms. "I don't know if that's a good thing or a bad thing." He rested a moment and rapped twice on the door. "I need assurance, regardless. I need to be certain that he doesn't know I exist. I need to feel safe."

Byrd cocked his head to the side as the door opened. "I realize this is minimum security jail, but you think you're ever really going to feel truly safe in here?"

"This is my second home, Byrd. Some enjoy the Cape. Some, a cabin in the woods." Michael stepped out of the room. He walked ahead of the guard to a door constructed of solid metal bars. He glanced to his right at a mural of a bright sun over a long meadow of cornstalks reaching for the sky. He looked over his shoulder and smiled back at Byrd. "See, Byrd. It's not so bad."

Byrd rolled his eyes.

Michael turned toward the bars as the guard unlocked the door. "Don't take any wooden nickels," he called back behind him.

Byrd sighed. There were few people he could trust without question. For now, he would tread carefully back in Lowell and keep his cards, however explosive, close to his chest. He felt an unease. The feeling had descended deep and taken up residence in his bones.

CHAPTER FOURTEEN

Jayne Ranney stepped through the front door of the apartment. She found her mother Margaret and Dawn Bridges, their neighbor, camped out on the couch amid chip bags, magazines, and peanut shells. An ashtray overflowed on the coffee table, and ash peppered the wide, wood surface.

Margaret stood with a sway and gestured to Jayne as the woman's drink splashed out over the rim of her glass. "You got money on you?"

"Some." Jayne walked toward the kitchen and dropped her book bag from her shoulder. She slung it over the back of a chair at the table and turned to the cabinet. She pulled out a small pot and a can of ravioli to heat for her dinner.

Margaret approached from behind and grasped Jayne harshly by the upper arm. "I need you to hit the market. There's a list over by Dawn."

Jayne looked over her shoulder to the couch. Dawn reclined, her girth spread over the width of two cushions.

Margaret tightened her hold on Jayne's arm and tugged hard. "Don't come back without my cigarettes."

Jayne nodded and dropped her eyes to her mother's grip. Margaret held fast and waited. Jayne raised her eyes and met her mother's stern expression. Margaret released the arm.

She returned to the living room, berating her daughter with a back turned. "Despite what may be going on in that head of yours, the Greek doesn't scare me in the slightest. I expect you to carry your weight around here and be home when I need you."

Jayne left the kitchen. She ignored the low rumble of hunger in the pit of her stomach and washed up in the bathroom sink. She combed tangles from her hair and counted each stroke in silence. She set the long strands back in a braid with care. She paused a moment to stare at her reflection. She knew full well the pulse of pain emanating from her arm was a precursor to unsightly bruising.

She returned to the kitchen, counting each footfall as a continuation of the numerical progression she started in her head in the bathroom. She drank a glass of water from the tap and grabbed up the grocery list on her way to the door. She exited the apartment and stopped at the small convenience store around the corner as the sun managed to send forth the last small crescents of light before setting.

The owner, standing over a counter ringed with penny candy, had sold cigarettes to Jayne since she was eight years old. Margaret set up an account that was to be settled every two weeks and had provided her with a note that first solo visit.

To Jayne, the proprietor was a lasting presence in her childhood, from administering to her skinned knee after a stray dog plowed her over, the shepherd snatching a chocolate coin from her hand as she stood outside the door, to the man attempting to hide his disappointment the many times Margaret sent Jayne in to do her bidding when Jayne knew full well the account was overdue. Even now, heat rose on Jayne's cheeks thinking on those awkward encounters. Times when she was essentially sent in to beg.

The man peered down from the raised floor behind the register, and Jayne felt like that small child once again. She paid for her purchase with cash and struck out for DeMoulas with her mind spinning. She was anxious since leaving the apartment, and her nerves continued to ratchet up. She scraped the soles of her shoes as she walked on the uneven sidewalk, while underfoot, from cracks and seams in concrete stones, tufts of weeds reached for the color spray on the sky.

Jayne reached DeMoulas and was hesitant to enter the market. The fact was, once her irrational, elusive fears reached their threshold, no compulsive count could slow the onset of a spell. Her very first since she began to work for Galen.

She entered the brightly lit store, and a familiar hot numbness bloomed in her stomach and radiated out with a tingle through her extremities. She worked her way down the aisles and paused in front of the dairy case along the wall. Jayne's senses were hyperaware. She was cognizant of the flicker of light above the rows of milk bottles, sounds of wheels on nearby carts, and the steady hum from the motor of the refrigeration unit. She stood tall to brace herself, using the shopping cart for support, and carried on. She located most of the items on Margaret's list and worked her way through the checkout, lightheaded and nauseous.

Once outside and with her arms full, Jayne paused, her eyes tearing in relief.

≈

Overburdened, Jayne returned to the apartment and walked in on a large group of people gathered to socialize with Margaret and Dawn. Jayne made it over to the kitchen table and set down the bags from the market. She opened the refrigerator and shelved a portion of the groceries before closing the door and opening a couple of the upper cabinets.

A tall body leaned into her from behind, pressing her up against the sharp edge of the counter. She slid over, only to be trapped by a pair of long arms at either side. Jayne pushed back, getting nowhere, and tensed from head to toe on feeling beard stubble on the exposed skin under her left ear.

"Who do we have here?" he said.

"Back off or I'll scream."

"To who?"

"My mother. Now get off me."

"Babe, she didn't even turn her head when you walked in the door. I saw you, though. You going to offer me some milk and cookies?" He chuckled into her ear and took a deep breath with his nose in her hair.

She closed her eyes and felt one of his hands move to her waist. One of his legs moved between hers, and more weight pressed against her. Jayne swung an elbow back in warning, into the man's side. "Please, get off me. What is it with you guys?"

He slowly stepped away, unfazed by her jab. Jayne listened to the scrape of chair legs as he sat down at the table. She turned, taking in the man as he pulled a plastic baggie of marijuana and a small pack of papers from his shirt pocket.

"See this?" Jayne said. She motioned in a large arc with her finger pointed toward the floor. "My space. All my space."

He shrugged.

Jayne sneezed into her elbow. She breathed back in. "What are you, thirty?" she asked.

"Twenty-eight, sweet cheeks."

Jayne nodded and leaned back on the counter. "Change up that wardrobe and maybe you'll land someone without having to be a total creep about it. Someone age-appropriate."

He looked down at his clothes as he sprinkled dry, crushed leaves into two layers of cigarette paper. "What? I look good."

"Where'd you get the crazy idea that plaid pants were a good fit for you?"

"I'm a little offended by your tone."

"Suck it up." She pulled the remaining items from the last bag. She put the carton of cigarettes away. She folded up the paper bags and stowed them under the kitchen sink. "And what's with the lifts?"

"Huh?"

"The platform shoes. You expecting to challenge Havlicek to a jump ball after the party?"

He stopped in his tracks, the rolled joint suspended between his fingers. He turned his head and raised his voice. "Yo, Margaret. This kid of yours is being mean to me."

Jayne smirked. She glanced to the foot of the stairs before choosing to walk past the revelers and make her way out the front door instead. Her bedroom had no lock, and there was no way she trusted the style-challenged beast in the kitchen to leave her be.

She let the screen door slam shut on her departure. She raced off the step and was soon in the alley beside the Skillet. Jayne made her way to the rear of the building and banged with the side of her fist on the back door. A blond with cleavage to the breastbone and nails of deep burgundy pushed open the door and stepped back for Jayne to enter.

"Tao here?" Jayne said.

"Up front."

"Thanks."

The place was busy. Jayne shouldered her way through the crowd, and her nerves became rattled in the cacophony of the space. She stood at the far end of the bar and moved behind when Tao crooked his finger in her direction.

He set a draft in front of a patron and threw a towel from the shelf, up over his shoulder. "You shouldn't be in here right now, Jayne." He reached down into a stainless-steel cooler to shovel some ice into a glass. "Galen told me you had nothing to drop back today."

Jayne sighed. She waited for Tao to pour a 7 and 7. She absently laid her palm across her midsection for comfort.

Tao served the drink, wiped his hands on the towel, and reached out to tug once on Jayne's braid. "Talk to me, Mouse. Why you here?"

"I thought I could barback for you or something. Maybe hang out in Galen's office? Margaret's got friends over."

"Can't do it, Jayne. The ABC hit over on Lakeview Avenue two hours ago. We don't need a reason for them to be sniffing around if they make it over this way tonight."

Across from them at the bar, a man mumbled a few words to himself. He got up to use the men's room and tipped his beer over with an elbow. Tao swiftly pulled Jayne to the side, and she gasped. She had come up on her toes as he steered her by the arm out of the way of the overspill. Tao let go and lightly circled her wrist. He carefully lifted the sleeve of her loose jersey.

The welt, on pale skin, showed a clear impression of Margaret's fingers. Tao's head lifted, and his eyes scanned the crowd. Jimmy Tens was across the room, leaning with an elbow on the back of a booth. He appeared to be imparting wisdom to the couple seated within.

Tao barked out his name over the din of those gathered, and Jimmy's head came up like a shot. He gave a wink to Tao before turning and clapping the man at the table on the back. Jimmy walked with a heavy step toward the end of the bar as the couple's eyes followed his departure. He gave a quick pull up on the waistband of his jeans. His work boots, unlaced and splattered with white paint, shifted with each step. The army jacket he wore like a second skin showed severe signs of wear at the elbows and around the collar.

Tao walked Jayne to the end of the bar with a hand to her lower back. He leaned over and got closer to Jimmy's ear. "There's no game tonight. Bring Jayne upstairs and get her settled. There should be Aspirin in the bathroom medicine cabinet, and I need you to take a close look at her arm."

Tao placed his warm palm on the side of Jayne's head, smoothing her hair before tugging lightly, once more, on her braid. "Try to get some sleep up there. I'll wake you as soon as my shift ends. You going to be all right?"

Jayne nodded.

Jimmy reached out and clasped her hand. "I got this, Tao."

Jayne opened her mouth to offer thanks to Tao, but his back was turned. He had stepped away to address the growing queue at the taps.

Jimmy led Jayne down the hallway as people parted the way. He held her hand until they stood in front of the couch in the apartment above. "Roll up your sleeves."

Jayne slowly submitted to the request.

"Sit. I'll be right back," he said.

"I'm fine."

Jimmy pointed to the couch and Jayne sat, letting her head rest back. He returned with the Aspirin and a handkerchief filled with ice. He sat beside her, raised her sleeve, and clasped her hand. He turned it from side to side to inspect the mark on her arm. He placed the ice pack down gently to soothe Jayne's hurt. He reached for her opposite hand and had her hold the cold compress as he leaned forward for the bottle of pills. "Who did this?"

"Margaret."

Jimmy shook his head. "I know full well you're able to defend yourself. Why can't you do it with your mother?"

Jayne shrugged.

He stood and went to the kitchen. He returned with a glass of water and set it down on the short table in front of her. "Anything else happen to you tonight?"

Jayne yawned wide before responding. "Nope."

"Keep the ice on it a bit longer, take the Aspirin, and try to sleep." He pointed to the floor. The muffled sounds were constant and caused a small vibration in the apartment floor. "Hear that? It will be like counting sheep. I'll grab a blanket for you from the other room and lock up tight before I go. Use the line there to call down to the bar if you need Tao.

He'll be up in a few hours."

Jayne toed off her shoes by the heels and lifted her legs up under her to get comfortable.

CHAPTER FIFTEEN

Jimmy Tens entered at the front of the Cape Cod–style home in Dracut. He walked over to the entrance to the kitchen and leaned on the doorjamb. He had a distaste for the wallpaper. Squares of pastoral scenes clashed with the light blue of the oven door.

A woman washed dishes at the sink across the room. She stared out the window in front of her, to the backyard. Her hair was tied in a loose bun. When she turned to set a dish in the rack, Jimmy followed the line of her neck with his eyes. She wore a cotton blouse and a wraparound skirt that tied in a bow at her hip. She stood with her bare feet spread at the toes, her heels in, speaking to the many grueling years of ballet lessons she was subjected to as a child.

When her eyes moved again to the window, Jimmy took one step to his right to share her reflection in the pane of glass.

She jumped and dropped the coffee cup in her hand back into the sudsy water. "Jesus. You scared me half to death. How long have you been standing there?"

Jimmy walked forward. He placed a palm on her hip and eased her over toward the refrigerator. He reached down and opened the cabinet under the sink. He pulled out a bag the size of a shaving kit. "Only long enough to appreciate the view," he said.

Jimmy and Veronica Nowak had an unconventional relationship, one that began well before he left for Vietnam. Jimmy stayed at the house one or two nights a week. He took use of one of the bedrooms in the apartment above the bar the rest of the time. Only Galen and Tao knew of his whereabouts on those off nights, but only so they could reach out to find him when needed.

When Jimmy went off to war, Veronica was employed as a nurse at Saint Joseph's Hospital. She was now head nurse of her shift. And although it was never discussed at length, the two chose not to follow social norms and settle down to raise a family.

Jimmy reached over and pulled the tea towel from the door of the oven. He laid it down on the table and opened his kit.

"You going to ruin another one of my towels?" she asked.

He reached into his jacket and pulled his gun from its holster under his arm. He set it down on the table.

Veronica leaned back on the sink and brushed a loose hair away from her eye. "Can you send that kid over again to cut the lawn? I stepped over a garter snake on the path outside. The taller the grass gets, the closer they get to the house."

"He'll be here tomorrow," Jimmy replied. "Temps are dropping. Snake was probably just laying out in the sun. They're harmless."

"Not a comfort." She reached for her large purse on a chair under the phone on the wall. She extracted a small cardboard carton of vials wrapped in plastic and four packs of needles. She set them down beside him on the table.

"I told you—I don't want you taking chances with that stuff," he said. "I can stock myself." He poured oil onto a square of linen cloth from the kit. "You could lose your job."

She pulled two beer bottles from the refrigerator and sat down across the table. She opened one for him. "They're only painkillers, samples mostly, from distributors. No one's going to say anything. Hell, I sing on the docs medicating themselves at work and it would clear out half the surgical wing."

Jimmy looked down to concentrate on cleaning his gun. He was meticulous about keeping his weapon clean after being bogged down in rain and muck for his tour. He learned fast and hard, a clean weapon was an operational weapon.

"Can you stay the night?" she asked.

Jimmy nodded.

She took a drink of beer and curled her arm up to rest the bottle at her shoulder. "I can wash the clothes on you when I throw in a load. Although I don't know how many more washings that coat can go through before it disintegrates."

He took a long drink of his own beer and winked at her. His visits to the home helped to ease him. Especially when he had too many ruminating thoughts swirling around in his head. He watched as Veronica stood and stepped over to the refrigerator. She pulled out a plate that held a heel of a meatloaf and a small baked potato. She grabbed a knife from the drawer and cut the meat into slices.

"I'm not hungry," he said.

"You'll eat. You need to put some meat on your bones."

"That your medical opinion?"

"You lose any more weight, you're not going to have energy. To get up to whatever it is you need to get up to."

He turned his head back to his task and pushed a small bronze bore brush down the barrel of the gun. His woman was a keeper. She worked hard and convinced him she knew the man he was underneath. Knew the troubled man he was when he returned from Vietnam. And she never once pressured him to change. Never once asked him to meet her expectations.

He knew in his heart that when they were together, they were the best of themselves.

≈

Galen finished the last dregs of coffee in his cup and looked over as Tao entered the office. Tao sat down on the couch, stretched his legs, and ran a hand through his long hair.

Galen rocked his chair back on its springs. "You going to tell me what happened here last night? Because Jimmy was out there in the bar, not ten minutes ago, behaving like he wants to take someone to the woodshed. Even after a good night's sleep. You want to fill me in?"

"Jayne's mother bruised up our girl's arm. Probably came close to pulling it out of its socket, from the way it looks."

"Where is she?"

"I left her out front sitting with Brendan. So we could talk."

Galen rocked forward and pushed his cup to the side. "Check with Jimmy. Make sure he doesn't go over and deal with Margaret Ranney before speaking with me."

Tao sat up and leaned his forearms on his thighs. "Galen. I'm keeping her."

"Keeping her? Jayne? What, like a puppy?"

Tao rolled his eyes.

Galen eased off his glasses. He laid them down on the desk. "You going to get up and drive her to school in the mornings?"

Tao shrugged.

"You going to be making her pancakes? Asking about her day? Buying her lady things and taking her for trips to the zoo?"

"Galen, she's not getting that now."

"Margaret could cause trouble. She's got to be collecting from the state, and there's no way she's giving up that check without a fight. You'll need to go over there and let her know we won't fool with her welfare." Galen pinched the bridge of his nose between his thumb and first finger. The phone on his desk rang, and he picked up. He asked the caller to wait and set the receiver on his shoulder. "For now, head out and grab some ice.

Bar's running low."

Tao stood and pulled his keys from his front pocket.

Galen nodded once in acceptance. "Jayne can work her route as usual. Let her use upstairs if she's waiting for one of you to drop her back to your place. Have a spare key made and tell Carol Anne to teach her how to fix food for the guys. It'll give her something more to do."

Tao smirked. "Keep her off the streets."

Galen was stone-faced. "Jayne agree to stay with you?"

"She will."

CHAPTER SIXTEEN

Tao poured a fresh pint of beer for Brendan and slid over the saltshaker with the side of his hand before stepping back. He took his wallet from his back pocket and pulled out two receipts to turn over to Galen for reimbursement. The bar phone rang. Tao grabbed a pen and a napkin in haste. He answered on the third ring. "Go."

"Tao?" Jayne said, her voice soft and thready.

"Where are you, kid?"

"Home."

"You're at the apartment? What are you doing there? You were supposed to come here straight from school." He pushed the pen behind his ear. "Jayne? You sound funny. Your mother at you again?"

"No. She's dead."

Tao reacted instantly. He took advantage of the long cord and walked to the hook on the wall to grab up his leather jacket. "Jayne, I hear voices in the background. Who's there with you?" Tao gestured with his thumb for Brendan to get up from his stool and step behind the bar.

Jayne's voice returned to the line, muffled as if she was cupping the receiver. "Cops. Ambulance guys. They're climbing all over each other in here."

"Stay put. I'm on my way." Tao hung up the phone. He pulled on his jacket as he mirrored the expression of concern on Brendan's face. "Can you cover until Galen comes out?"

"You can count on me, chief. What's going on?" Brendan adjusted

125

the cap on his head and made his way around the end of the bar.

Tao eased by him. "I need to get over to Jayne. If the phone rings, answer and tell them to call back in ten." He walked down to the office. He reached the door, and Galen lifted his head from an accounting book on his desk.

"What?"

"Margaret Ranney's dead."

"What? How?"

Tao shrugged.

"Where's Jayne?" Galen asked.

"She's there. At the apartment."

Galen stood and reached behind his chair for his coat. Tao held up a hand, palm out.

"No. Stay. The place is crawling with cops."

Galen reached over to pick up the phone receiver. "Too much to hope for a simple slip and fall in the tub, huh? Where's Jimmy?"

"No idea."

"I'll get a line on him while you're gone."

Tao left the office. He booked for the front door with nary a glance at the bar, hit the street, ran past his truck, across Market Street, and through the small lot of the Holy Trinity Church. When he made his way through a row of apartments, he saw two men packing up an ambulance, two police cruisers, and one unmarked sedan. Tao walked toward the apartment door as the coroner's station wagon rolled down the street toward them.

The officer standing point wore a serious expression and glared at Tao. "Who're you?"

"Tao Mann. I'm here for Jayne Ranney. She's staying with me."

The officer looked at him with suspicion but held the door so Tao could enter. Tao shouldered his way between a plainclothes detective and another officer to find Jayne on the floor of the kitchen with her back leaning on the door of the refrigerator. The two men stepped farther toward the center of the living room, away from the front door.

"What's she doing on the floor?" Tao asked them.

"We tried to get her up into a chair, but she won't budge," the detective said.

Tao turned to Jayne and resisted an urge to pull her up and into his arms. Instead he slid his back down the refrigerator beside her and rested his forearms on his knees. "You okay?"

"Nope." She rested her head on his shoulder. "Thanks for coming."

"Any time." Tao looked up at the two in the living room. "Can I take her out of here?" He waited for a response that did not arrive and threw an arm around Jayne's shoulders.

≈

Officer Byrd White entered the apartment after a nod to his fellow officer.

The uniform followed him in. "What are you doing here? Thought you were on nights."

"I got a call," Byrd said. He pointed to a rental unit across the courtyard of O'Brien Terrace, one with a small American flag on a short pole jutting out beside the door. "Got a cousin who lives there. She's good people. Keeps me apprised of the goings-on. And word spreads like fire through this place. I thought I could lend a hand."

"What, like an interpreter? Far as I know, they're all speaking English in there," the officer said, waving his thumb. "The sergeant's going to go apeshit if he finds out you pulled up in your own car. You even sign in at the station?"

"No. Haven't had a shower yet either, so step aside." Byrd stopped farther inside the door.

In the living room, the rug was pulled up at one corner and out from under a side of the couch. The couch appeared to have been moved, angled more to the kitchen than the front of the room. A few of the kitchen cupboards were open and their contents spilled on the counter and scattered on the floor. Among the debris sat a girl he assumed was Michael Ranney's sister, a child he had not seen since she was waist-high. Joining her on the floor was a rough-looking man with a long scar marring his face. And, if Byrd was to guess, a lineage of no fewer than three nationalities. The man turned his head to where Byrd was standing and nodded once in acknowledgment of his presence.

Byrd took a moment to turn back to the officer at the door. "She find the body?"

"No. She walked in from school right before we arrived. A neighbor, Mrs. Bridges, already found the tenant and phoned it in." The man let out a short, awkward laugh. "I had to hustle the woman out of here. Found her staring down at the kid as if the girl was intentionally blocking access to the fridge."

Byrd cocked his head, not grasping the significance.

"Mrs. Bridges is a large lady," the man said.

Byrd nodded and approached the kitchen.

"When can I take her home?" Tao asked.

"Isn't this her home?"

"No. She's staying with me." Tao eased his way up to stand and offered his hand. "The name's Tao. Can you tell me what's happened with Jayne's mother?"

Byrd shook his hand. "Byrd White." He glanced up at the ceiling. "I just got here myself. I have a few questions." He looked around them at the small apartment. "Let's you and I move into the bathroom there for a moment."

Tao looked down to Jayne, and she nodded her acceptance. Tao followed Byrd to the bathroom and sat inside, on the edge of the tub. He gave Byrd his full attention.

"First—how are you related?" Byrd said.

"I'm not."

"And the girl's staying with you?"

"That's right."

"How do you know the family?"

"Margaret's son Michael. After he went back to jail, I kept an eye on the family, and recent circumstances had me stepping in and giving Jayne a place to live."

Byrd adjusted his holster to stop it from digging in his side as he leaned on the sink. "You hung around with Michael?"

"Hell, no. Cleaned up after some of his messes, though. Big relief he got sent up again, actually. So, you going to tell me how the woman upstairs bought it?"

"Suicide—pills, I've been told. Haven't delved into it with my colleagues yet, though."

Tao shook his head. "She doesn't seem the type," he said.

"What do you mean?"

"Hard woman, that one. Mean streak a mile long and her best partying days ahead of her. She had no responsibilities that she accepted. No job—rent subsidized. Food stamps to keep her cupboards filled. Maybe a hand job for a neighbor here and there to keep cash in her pocket for another bottle. What's someone like that jumping ship for? For the brief time we were acquainted, I never once saw an expression of shame or empathy or kindness on her face. You need a conscience to contemplate suicide. You need to be able to feel the wrong." Tao sighed deeply before continuing. "Some of the best people commit suicide, man. Ever hear, 'How could they do that and not think about the people left behind?' when, more than likely that's all they're thinking about before the act. I just can't see that woman checking out. She didn't have the heart."

"Regardless. Once I confirm your arrangement with the daughter, I'll get it cleared for you to take her. But right now, I need to relay a word of caution. I have a problem with the call of suicide myself. And I need you to promise not to let the girl out of your sight. Not until I can clear up a few things."

"What's going on?"

"I can't get into it here." Byrd handed Tao his notepad, opened to a blank page, and a pen. "Write down your address and phone number."

Tao scribbled down the information.

"Where can I find you when you're not home?" Byrd asked as he took back the notepad and slipped it into the pocket of his uniform.

"The Skillet—I bartend."

"You work for the Greek?"

Tao nodded.

"I'm assuming, then, you people have a good grasp on protecting the kid," Byrd said.

"No worries."

A knock brought Tao to his feet, and the door to the bathroom swung wide, hitting the wall with a bang.

The detective from out front, Daniel Solomon, stood in his rumpled suit coat, his tie stained with coffee or tea, his white collared shirt yellow with age. Near retirement, the man was thoroughly lax in his appearance. "Officer White, may I speak to you outside?"

"Of course, sir," Byrd said.

Tao stepped a foot forward as Byrd made his way out the door.

"You stay put," Detective Solomon said to Tao as he pointed to the bathtub.

"Why?"

"Sit the hell down." Solomon motioned to the officer he had been speaking with in the living room to stand guard at the entrance of the bathroom.

Byrd followed his superior to the front of the apartment and out the door.

"Officer White, care to explain to me why you're conducting a closed-door meeting with a civilian?" Solomon asked.

"Only ascertaining the minor's guardianship."

"Did you discuss anything pertaining to the deceased? Because if it ain't goddamn obvious, I'm in charge. And I'd appreciate you not conducting interviews without my knowledge or consent."

"We were just discussing the daughter, sir. Tao's been housing the girl."

"Next time you pull someone aside under my watch, I'll have your ass. And if I find out you haven't turned over your findings to me, if I find out that man had anything to add to my investigation, including the deceased's state of mind in recent days, and you failed to disclose the information—you'll cease to exist in this department."

"Yes, sir."

"We're about to wrap up here. But I want a complete written report from you. And get that piece of shit you have holed up in the bathroom off my scene. Now. I don't care if you two used to play tiddlywinks together. You know better than to allow a civilian privileged access or information."

"I'll take care of him. And, sir? With all due respect, may I ask if you've reached a conclusion as to cause of death? Are there avenues we can pursue? Something to explain the obvious signs of someone riffling through the apartment."

"My investigation isn't over. I haven't made a set ruling on the cause of death," Solomon said, reaching for a lighter in his coat pocket and snapping the cover open and closed. "The vic could have very well been searching for something in a desperate state or created the mess in anger. These people don't have money. There's nothing much to steal, but the TV's sitting there in the living room. There are a handful of bills, about fifteen dollars, still sitting on the woman's bureau. And, plainly, for you to suggest I may not be conducting a thorough investigation is damn insulting."

"Sorry, sir."

"If you have concerns, place them in writing with your report. And be in my office first thing tomorrow morning."

"But, sir, I work late shift tonight."

"Pulling a double?"

"No. But I'm on at ten tonight," Byrd said.

Solomon pulled out a cigarette from a pack in his coat pocket. "I'll be sure not to keep you long, then. Be there 8:00 a.m., sharp."

"Yes, sir. Understood."

Byrd stepped back into the apartment and collected Tao. "Be sure to remember what we discussed," he imparted.

Tao nodded. They entered the kitchen, and Tao reached his hand out to help Jayne up from the floor. "Time to go."

On the stairs, the two men from the coroner's office who had bagged Margaret's body and strapped the woman to a gurney now struggled to maneuver down the narrow steps and up over the railing in a sharp angle to the door. They each grabbed a handle on the side and stood the dead woman up, near vertical. Tao turned his body to block Jayne from the sight. He placed his hand on her back and ushered her toward the front door. Byrd stepped around them and held the door ajar with one long arm. The officer that had been standing point was beside him. The man let out a quick bark of laughter that he attempted to conceal with a cough as he watched the extraction. Byrd cuffed the back of his head with the palm of his hand and received an expression of offense and anger in return.

≈

Tao walked Jayne back over to Market Street. He was desperately in need of a joint. So, without words, he steered them across the road to the convenience store for rolling papers. Two minutes at the counter and they were back on the sidewalk. Tao stepped off the curb to his truck and grabbed his weed from the glove compartment. He closed the door and turned, glancing over Jayne's head to the side alley. Sally James was down on her knees in front of a john. It was another shock to his system. It had Tao gritting his teeth. "What the devil? Sally, move that shit out of here."

Sally stood swiftly. She wiped the back of her hand across her mouth. "Sorry, Tao. I swear, we didn't come from inside."

Sally's trick adjusted himself and with a tuck and a roll he carefully zipped up his pants. "You could at least let her finish, man. I'm dying here."

"Tough shit. Pay the lady and get lost," Tao said.

"She got her money already."

Tao motioned with his head to the street. "You driving?"

The man leaned his back on the brick wall. He tucked in his shirt and buckled his belt. He pointed to a blue sedan. "That's me."

"Why do you have her on her knees, then? There's frigg'n glass down there. What's wrong with you, man?"

The john shrugged. "I pick my wife and kid up in half an hour. Out here seemed the better choice."

Tao shook his head as Sally made her leave to the mouth of the alley. Tao motioned for Jayne to walk ahead of him, and they approached the front of the bar. He held the door open and looked over at Sally as she walked backward away from the building. Her expression was one of guilt and remorse. Tao nodded once in acceptance of her silent apology, the breach of boundary evident. He did not need to mention it again.

≈

Galen heard a welcome commotion. Jimmy Tens walked in the back door of the bar as Tao and Jayne arrived in the front. The two men gathered with Galen in his office, prepared for a debriefing and to discuss their concerns for Jayne. She sat out at the bar under Brendan's watchful eye.

Galen leaned back, causing the springs of his chair to protest. "I'll start. They found an empty, unmarked bottle of what they assume to have been pills by the bed, along with a near-empty bottle of vodka. They're going to test the powder in the pill bottle to identify the type of drug Margaret ingested."

"Good riddance," Jimmy said, tugging on his beard.

Galen's eyebrows rose. "You have something to tell us, Jimmy?"

"No. I was with our friends at North Station. Just saying, don't think anyone's going to miss the woman."

"Did our friends try to raise the number again?" Tao asked.

"Nope. Not this week. Bastard was too happy relaying some anecdote about a broad. I laughed at the appropriate times. Then hightailed it out."

Galen picked up a pen from his desk to fiddle with. "Margaret had a bruise. It ran from her shoulder across her collar bone," he said.

"That's telling," Jimmy said.

Galen tossed down the pen. "My thought exactly. Could be someone held her down and made her swallow the pills."

Jimmy again bothered his beard. "Doing her that way is going to take time. It's not like a hit to the head. She has to lose consciousness, and even then, depending on what she swallowed, it could be twenty minutes. An hour before she succumbs."

Tao leaned forward on the couch. "Say that's how it went down. How did the doer know Jayne wasn't going to be there or walk in at any time?"

Galen and Jimmy spoke at once. "He didn't."

Galen set the springs to squeaking again. "What did you get from over there?"

Tao stood, too agitated to remain seated any longer. "They can write off the bruise as falls from her drinking. There has to be others on her body from bumping into walls and furniture. The mess of the place didn't seem to raise any eyebrows." He leaned his shoulder on the wall beside him. "But a cop pulled me aside. He's got something for us."

Intense interest sparked in Galen's eyes. "What is it?"

Tao shrugged. "He told me he wasn't sold on Margaret killing herself. But he's keeping the details close to the vest. Or he just didn't have time to fill me in. He wants us to keep Jayne close, not let her out of our sight. He's warning us that someone may be out there, lurking in the dark."

"What's his name, this cop?" Galen asked.

"Byrd White. He's street-level. Wears the uniform of a beat cop, but he could be driving patrol."

"I know the family," Jimmy said.

"White's a pretty popular name," Tao said.

"How many people name a kid Byrd? One of the brothers went over to 'Nam a year or so ahead of me. He didn't make it home," Jimmy said. "Byrd I know by sight. But I don't think I've ever spoken to him."

Galen sighed and picked up the pen once more. "Get me his address, and I'll pay him a visit. I'd rather not send feelers out downtown, because I don't want anyone to know we're going to be talking to this guy."

"You sure that's the right call, Galen?" Jimmy said. "I could get in there and be there to greet him when he gets home."

Galen gave a quick smile. "He set our meeting in motion with Tao today. I appreciate the offer of your interrogation skills, Jimmy, but let's give the guy a chance." He reached into the side drawer of his desk and pulled out the items for Jayne's run. "Get a spare piece, James. One not coming back to you. I want us to shore up and have one at our disposal. This thing with Margaret today, it's not going anywhere good." Galen handed Jimmy the satchel. "For now, knock this out for me, will you?"

"I want your word someone's on Jayne," Jimmy said.

"She's covered. Tao will need you to relieve him, so work your way back here." Galen motioned with his chin to the satchel in Jimmy's hand. "There are only two stops in there. I'll have Carol Anne cover a few of Tao's shifts starting tonight." Galen leaned back in his chair. "If the two of you need to see to something, I want you dropping Jayne back to me. We stay with her until we figure out what's what. Keep her away from that apartment."

Tao nodded. "What do we do about burying her mother? I don't think Michael's up to the task from his digs."

Galen stood. "Jayne's call. Let's get this business settled, and I'll find out what she wants to do."

≈

In the morning, after two brutally strong cups of coffee, Byrd White arrived at the station and sat on a bench in the locker room in the basement. He re-read his report and, satisfied, tore off a carbon copy for himself and stowed it in his locker. He walked the two flights of stairs to Detective Solomon's office. He knocked on the frame of the door as it sat ajar.

"Sit," Solomon said.

The old man's desk was cluttered. A stack of folders perched on the corner, high enough to be listing precariously. Byrd sat in one of the two facing chairs and slipped his report onto the only exposed surface in front of him.

Solomon leaned back in his chair. "You all squared from yesterday?"

Byrd nodded.

Solomon slid a legal pad of paper from his hands onto the desk. "Because you may not have been outright insubordinate, but the careless-ness in your casual manner, speaking with a member of the public on an active scene, needs to be addressed."

"Sir? My private discussion with Mr. Mann was with no malin-tent. I was only attempting to ease his concerns for the daughter of the deceased."

"See, that's the problem right there," Solomon responded. "That word 'private' shouldn't even be in your vocabulary as it pertains to the job. You reach my position, maybe. But where you sit, this here," Solomon gestured between them with his finger, "for you, this is a group effort. Haven't you heard the talk from MacPhail? We're to be a cohesive unit. I can't have young officers running roughshod over my investigations with no authority, no direction."

Byrd felt heat crawl up his neck, and he did his best to school his expression.

Solomon sighed and smoothed his tie with the palm of his hand, the same tie he had worn the previous day. "The next of kin is Michael Ranney. The son. Sitting pretty up in Billerica. We're having prison authorities give notification." He leaned back farther in his chair. "The death has officially been ruled an overdose. Of course, I will review your report, and if there are any observations I deem necessary additions to my findings, they will go into the file." He pulled the writing pad back toward him. He ignored Byrd's report, choosing to read his own notes. He reached up and fixed his eyeglasses more squarely on his face. "That's all for now, Officer White. You're dismissed."

"Thank you, sir." Byrd exited the office. He would stop at the gym on Lawrence Street to hit the bag and work out the tension building between his shoulders. Then head home to some much-needed shut-eye.

CHAPTER SEVENTEEN

Byrd experienced yet another disrupted sleep as he lay on the couch in his living room. He dreamed of an event that seemed once again to play out in real time.

On a moonless night in a past winter, on the tail end of a shift, Byrd walked his route with a partner. The two men turned the corner to the station and looked up to see fire engulfing a four-story apartment building. The building butted up against a downtown canal. Four people jumped to escape the flames and landed in the canal that night. They jumped in only the clothes they wore to bed and plunged into freezing water, fortunate that the sluggish flow in the canal kept the surface from turning solid with ice.

Byrd stood stunned a moment and watched the last jumper leap: a young woman in her underwear, her arms down at her sides, palms flat as if to catch herself on the water's surface. The sound when she hit reverberated through Byrd. He shed his gun and gun belt. He passed them over to his partner as emergency vehicles pulled up to the location.

Byrd jumped feetfirst into the canal and experienced a shock on entering the water that stole his breath. Over the next crucial minutes, he did his best to assist Fire and Rescue to pull each victim of the fire from the dark waters, over to the stone-block side wall of the canal to be hoisted up and over the rail.

Byrd went under the shimmering surface that reflected the flames, repeatedly, in search of the last victim—the woman. The sight of her falling figure replayed in his head as he searched near blind for any movement. He reached out, attempting to feel for an arm or a leg. His wool uniform was heavy and made it harder each time to reach the surface to breathe.

A rescue squad diver appeared beside him. He told Byrd emphatically to get out of the water. Byrd accepted a line thrown to him from above and walked his feet up the wall. He was helped over the edge by numerous hands. The night sergeant on the fire stared down at Byrd once he lay on the ground. He told him to walk back to the station, a short distance away.

Byrd's uniform froze stiff in that short distance. The last few hundred yards proved to be a struggle as he shook from the beginning stages of hypothermia. He entered the station and was hustled to the back office, stripped down, and given a blanket. One of the men broke into a lieutenant's office and absconded with a bottle of whiskey from a desk drawer. They poured the amber liquid into Byrd's gullet.

The diver eventually stopped into the station, heralding news as Byrd recovered. One man had survived. Out of the four civilians who went into the water, one man lived to see the morning. The woman, though, the young lady who Byrd dived for so desperately, was found near the bottom of the canal. In death, she clutched a tree limb that was anchored to its dead trunk against the base of the wall. The diver had needed to pry her hand free to lift her lifeless body to the surface.

There was a hard knock on Byrd's door. It shook him from the memory of that night and brought him back to the here and now. And he sat up on his couch, grateful.

Byrd made it across the room as another knock sounded. He opened the door and stared sleepily at Galen Stathakis as the man stood casually on his front stoop. "I'm not going to ask how you found me."

"You got coffee?" Galen tucked his keys in his coat pocket and entered the house as if on a welcome.

Byrd followed into the kitchen to start a pot. Galen sat down on a stool at the counter. He glanced around him and took in the first floor. A house without a kitchen set of table and chairs. A living room that held no touches of warmth, no rug, no drapes.

"You live lean," Galen said.

"My ex-wife cleared me out. I didn't fight her on anything. Just let her take the lot."

"Why?"

"She's shacked up with a guy I came up with in the academy."

Galen patted the pocket of his shirt. "Shame."

Byrd nodded. "I copped on to their affection for one another at my brother's funeral, of all places." He crossed his arms and tucked his hands under his armpits.

Galen chose not to respond. He sat quiet as if waiting for Byrd to continue.

Byrd obliged. "People don't know what to say to you at those things. You lose a brother, someone real close, they leave you alone if you want it that way. And that was me. Sitting in my corner of the room after the cemetery. My folks and sister holding court. Me, I'd get someone dropping me food and trying to get me to eat. A beer and they'd move on. The whole time I had my eyes on the two of them. Even before that, at the wake, across the grave. Don't know why, but I was focused. I saw it. The looks that held too long."

"How could you be sure?"

"I set down my beer. Stepped over the plate of food I left on the floor and walked out on the deck. There were a few of the guys standing around laughing at some lame joke. And I laid the guy out. Used all the pent-up pain and anger at losing my twin brother and broke his jaw. Rang his bell when he hit his head on the deck. My wife, she comes scrambling through the sliding door. Pushing people this way and that to get down beside the guy. And one look up at me sealed it. You would've thought I kicked her new puppy across the room."

"She was no good anyway—stepping out on you."

"What a wonderful way to call my wife a whore."

"Ex-wife."

Byrd turned and pulled down coffee cups from his kitchen cabinets. He handed Galen one and kept the one with a jagged chip in the lip for himself. "Shall we get to the matter at hand?"

"Any news on Margaret Ranney?" Galen inquired.

"It's an overdose. Book's closed."

"You spoke to my man, Tao, yesterday. You suggested something different."

Byrd leaned over and pulled a glass bottle of milk from the refrigerator. "I don't even know what to call you. Is it 'the Greek' or Mr. Stathakis?"

"Galen."

Byrd nodded. "I'm pulling a few threads on my own on this. But I pull the wrong one or pull it out too far, the ramifications could be big. Bigger than finding an alcoholic, abusive, middle-aged mother put out of her misery."

"How'd you know there was abuse?"

"My cousin lives cross the courtyard."

Galen looked down at his large hands stretched out on the surface of the counter. "May I ask why you suggested we keep a close eye on Jayne? Does it have anything to do with that brother of hers?"

"Don't know if I can say."

"Let me fill you in on something. Michael Ranney's my godchild. I take that responsibility seriously. But he has the talent of attracting all manner of trouble. I'd like to say I've done my best with his father gone, but there is no saving someone who is reckless. And now that he's locked up, guaranteed not to sidle up to my bar, I figure he's contained." Galen lifted his head and looked Byrd in the eyes, inquiring.

"Michael's been speaking to me," Byrd said.

"What can you tell me?"

"I don't know. I don't know fully what I'm dealing with here. Michael's given me some names, and I've been using my resources. But the more we talk about this, the more rooting around I do, the more trips to Billerica I take, the more danger everyone is in."

"If this is about Michael, why'd they go after Margaret?"

"Maybe they couldn't reach him in there."

Galen smirked. "Everyone's reachable in there. And they're short-timers, so easier to get at."

"Then Michael's holding back on me. He's holding a card I can't read."

"I'll find out what I need to from Michael. One threat of cutting him off, and he'll fill me in on all of it."

"Cutting him off from what?" Byrd said.

Galen smiled. "Always the cop."

Byrd ran a hand over his short stubble of hair. "Don't want any of you forgetting who I am."

"Don't want you forgetting who I am either," Galen said. "We'll have no trouble if we keep the same aims."

"Which are?"

"Jayne Ranney. Safe."

Byrd sighed. "The farther this thing progresses, the more likely I'll need to change my profession."

"I'm not working on enough information to be agreeing or disagreeing with you. But you help us keep my girl safe, and I'll owe you."

"I'll do what I think is right, in my own judgment. At the end, we go back to the way things were. I'll pretend I have no knowledge of your activities. And you'll go back to seeing me as a harmless officer of the law."

A nod in return and Galen pushed his cup to the side of the sink. He got up from the stool and took his leave.

≈

Tao Mann sat across a small table from Michael Ranney in the large visitors' room of the BHC. A checkerboard-tiled floor lay under their feet. They were monitored closely by three guards, two inside and one in an office with a large window overlooking the room. It held an outside line and mechanisms to release the door lock to both the general population of the prison and the door used by visitors to reach a smaller anteroom.

Tao and Michael were seated close enough to others to overhear conversations. Complaints about meeting household bills and other responsibilities, questions of well-being, sharing of family news, and those relaying details of mundane tasks.

Michael had a week or so growth of hair on his face, and he scratched an itch near his ear. "You going to sit with me like this until they send me back to my cell, or you going to say something?"

"They tell you your mother's dead?"

"Yup." Michael waited again. He glanced over to Roy, who was visiting with his mother. The woman licked the tips of her fingers on one hand and reached across to smooth unruly bangs aside on Roy's forehead. Michael smiled and turned back to Tao.

"We need the name," Tao said. "The big guy wants more, but we'll work with a name."

Michael nodded. "When they told me she overdosed, I knew it was crap. I mean, there wasn't enough pills or the right type in my stash to do the damage. The worst she could manage was getting extra sleepy on a couple of ludes or speed out for an afternoon. Jayne can tell you if she got to them. And pills were never Margaret's thing. Imagining Margaret scoring on the Common is like imagining your parents having sex when you're a kid. You know?"

"The name."

"Tell Galen he's best not to get involved in this one. I've got a guy."

"You've got a guy? You stubborn twit. We know all about him, and if it was us, he'd be the last type of guy we'd reach out to for assistance."

Michael scratched again near his ear. "And I'm telling you, I've got this."

"You've got squat. What about your sister? Or are you like your mother and think of the kid as an afterthought."

The skin of Michael's neck turned red, and the color worked its way up his face. He took a moment to compose himself before responding.

"The name," Tao said.

"It might not be him. And if it is him, I had no idea he'd go after my family. Where does that get him? How's that supposed to work? You guys have no idea what this is. What good is it to have you running around in the dark? I can't get into this here, and I want to give my guy a chance to do what he can to get me information. Something to work with. I know I can't fully trust the man, but he's in the best position to help me out. And I think I made the right call." Michael took in a few calming breaths and closed his eyes for a moment before continuing. "The bastard's one sick puppy if he goes after my sister. I don't know how to process that thought. What more can I do? I came in here to steer away from the guy, and I thought I was safe. I thought he didn't know about me. He still might not."

"The name."

Michael leaned as far forward as he could without drawing the attention of a guard. "Tom Curry. He's FBI."

Tao's shoulders fell. "You're screwing with me."

"I wish I was. Do you see why I need to keep quiet on this? Keep it small?"

Tao stood and walked to the visitors' door. He nodded to the guard within and exited when the lock released. He left the room without glancing back.

≈

Tao unlocked his side door and turned on the lights in the mudroom before ushering Jayne into his home. The room was only heated with what warmth escaped from the kitchen through a small vent in the lower panel of the door. The fall nights were getting colder, and the dark descended a few minutes earlier each day.

They entered the house, and Jayne slung her book bag over the back of a chair. She refused to leave it behind at the bar, because she was used to keeping a close eye on it. Tao headed to his bedroom. He set his wallet on his bureau and adjusted the thermostat on his way back to the kitchen to check on food for dinner.

Jayne sat at the table, her ankles crossed and her hands wedged between her thighs for warmth. She peered out through the living room, out the large bay window, even though night had fallen. "You saw Michael today?"

Tao nodded as he pulled lettuce, cucumber, and a ripe tomato from a drawer in the refrigerator. The previous weekend, he had raked debris from his lawn and shored up a rock ledge on the far side of his garage. The physical work added pain to the exhaustion he felt now in his bones. He reached in a low cabinet for a bag of potatoes he planned to roast with a simple mix of olive oil, salt, and pepper.

"Is he okay?" she asked.

"He's fine. That brother of yours manages to be just fine. No matter what's coming down the river."

She watched as Tao chopped the potatoes into cubes as the oven heated. She stood and stepped forward to unwrap the lettuce on the counter. Tao reached in another cabinet and pulled out a colander for the sink. They took turns rinsing the potatoes and vegetables under cold water.

"What happens now?" Jayne asked.

Tao turned his head and saw the worry etched on her face. "Now? We eat and get some rest. Tomorrow and the next day, and the next, we talk. We figure it out together. You're not alone."

She found a knife, bowl, and cutting board with Tao pointing in direction. She prepared the salad. With the potatoes in the oven, Tao cut thick slices of cold ham from the refrigerator. The quiet between them was a comfort, and it continued throughout their meal.

In the hallway after the dishes were washed and the kitchen set to right, Tao put an arm around Jayne's shoulders and kissed her on the head. The kindness seemed appropriate given the events of the last couple days. Hopefully it eased some worry in Jayne and she was able to fall asleep wrapped in warm bedding. After her first night at the house, Tao had prepared and outfitted a room for her at the end of the hall.

CHAPTER EIGHTEEN

Officer White walked out of the guardroom at the police station, and the door squeaked behind him as it swung shut. He walked down the hall to the front of the station. Danny, the desk sergeant, barked out orders over the phone as he instructed an officer to get a wagon over to the Celtic Club because of a large brawl that had spilled out into the street. The scene was reported to be out of control.

"What is it?" Danny said to Byrd with the receiver still cradled to his ear.

Byrd pointed to a locked wooden cabinet along the wall. "I want to look at the logbook for November, last year," he said.

"What for?" Danny reached for the ring of keys at his hip and unclipped them from his belt before waiting for a response.

Byrd held out his hand. "I need to check for calls on a property across the river."

Danny shook his head and tossed his glut of keys the short distance to Byrd's palm. The sergeant opened the line on his conversation on the phone once again. He told the driver of the wagon to shake his tail and call if he needed more bodies to manage the crowd.

For a while Danny was distracted by a walk-in complaint and a series of calls answered with the sergeant's stern greeting. Byrd opened the cabinet and searched the books for November of '71. The information was recorded by date and was easy to locate. Deciphering the scrawl of entries was more of a challenge. But the longer he read over the lines, the more they began to come into focus. He could even make out shift changes by the time of entry and changes in handwriting. Not that any particular handwriting was any easier to read than another.

Byrd set the logbook he needed on top of the cabinet and thumbed through to November. On the fourth page, a short note was made on the same date Sergeant Ray Hamel was found in his kitchen. An anonymous call was placed to the station of a broken window and unsecured door at the George Chadwick School in Pawtucketville. There was no record that men were dispatched to the property on that date, probably due to the commotion at the house of one of their own.

Byrd found an additional entry on Friday the nineteenth. Two days after the call. Two portable police officers were sent to the Chadwick School to investigate. Byrd wrote down their names and the dates in his notepad. He was curious if a caller had phoned back to prompt the eventual response.

Byrd locked the cabinet after returning the book. He laid the keys down beside the desk sergeant, not wanting to disturb him mid-call. He made his way around the sergeant to the front of the desk and waited for the man to complete a call.

"You need me driving over and giving assistance at the club?" Byrd asked as Danny set the phone receiver into its cradle.

"No. If they aren't on their way back by now, I would have gotten the call. You find what you're looking for?"

"All set."

"Good. I may need you later. There are complaints of someone setting up camp in the woods on the bank of the river. Same spot I sent you to last month. Near the university's main campus. We've been getting calls about small fires and squawking about the look of the place."

"Fires to warm a can of beans and keep warm."

"Regardless of their attempts at domesticity, I need to roust them tonight. Get them to move off. Or at least a bit more downstream."

"I'll call in when I make it to University Avenue and Pawtucket."

"I can send the wagon when my driver's back."

"I'll see if they cooperate and let you know." Byrd closed the buttons on his uniform coat and lifted his collar before heading out the door.

≈

In the morning, Byrd caught a solid four hours of restful sleep, bunking down on the mattress on the floor of his bedroom instead of the couch. He left the house after dressing in civilian clothes and drove his car to the Cameo Diner, a favorite of his coworkers for a spot to rest and regroup during a shift. It was across the river from the station, at a far enough distance to avoid tripping over a supervisor or superior.

Byrd entered the diner and spotted Officer Carl Woodhouse as the man leered at a woman's ass. She was wiping down a cleared table. Byrd walked around her, down to the edge of the booth. "Woodhouse—got a minute?" He slid into the bench seat across from the man.

Woodhouse looked over and set his fork on his plate of bacon and eggs. "Make yourself comfortable," he said without a trace of sincerity.

Byrd smiled and turned over the downturned mug on his side of the table. He lifted it to signal for coffee. "I need to pick your brain for a second."

Woodhouse did not respond, only lifted his eyebrows and looked down his long nose.

"The Chadwick School. Last November, the nineteenth, a Friday."

"Last November," Woodhouse said, deadpan.

"You were sent over after a B and E was reported. A broken window at the school."

"Rings a bell."

"Can you tell me about it?"

"Simple callout. Nothing to report. We did a walk-through. Then called city DPW to put some plywood over the window and set a chain on a gym door to secure the place. What's the deal?"

"Nothing strike you about the call?"

"Byrd—you're a hump like me. What're you doing?"

Byrd shrugged and held his mug aloft as the waitress poured him some hot coffee.

Woodhouse adjusted the waist of this uniform pants with a thumb and pushed his plate to the center of the table. "We found a couple tools in the kitchen off the cafeteria, and there was damage to some ceiling tiles in the room. Other than that, there wasn't much to take. Most of it had been cleared out when the school closed its doors. The place had the same smell as when I was there as a kid." He crossed his arms on his chest. "Seriously, though. What's the interest?"

"You log the tools?" Byrd asked.

"Of course. Now that's all I have. Can you leave me in peace? I've ten minutes of my break left, and I'd rather not spend them talking shop."

≈

Byrd wiled away the day back at his house, unsettled and anxious. He harbored a deep, instinctive feeling that the off-book inquiries he was making were going to get himself or someone else hurt. But walking away now, from Michael Ranney, from suspicion of a corrupt federal agent, from letting the likely murder of a fellow officer sit fallow, not to mention the demise of a civilian in what could be said was in similarly staged-suicide fashion—was untenable.

He arrived at work early once again and made use of the permissions of his badge to access the evidence lockers. Items within were cataloged for their eventual use at trial or for shipment to storage on hitting a statutory date.

Another book and handwriting to decipher to get to a large manila envelope. The notes scribbled on the front contained a catalogue number, a location from where the evidence had been collected, and the date and signature of Officer Woodhouse, who had sealed the envelope. A further note on the back flap called out the lifting of fingerprints from a tool on the same date as the evidence file.

To Byrd, the note was a contradiction, because the envelope in his hand was light as air. Any contents had been taken, and no one had signed or initialed the log after the filing officer signed it into evidence. Byrd added his own name under Woodhouse's signature. He opened the envelope and noted on the front that it was empty upon inspection.

He moved out of the evidence room and opened a long, narrow drawer of fingerprint cards. He searched for the catalogue number of the George Chadwick B and E to see if a duplicate copy of prints was filed before dropping his head in defeat. Whatever had been filed no longer existed.

Any action Byrd took to register a complaint would be met with scrutiny. He was at a loss to conjure a plan. A path to follow to satisfy his need to bring whatever this was to conclusion. Signing in upstairs and getting on his route would be a welcome relief, but to think the situation would work its way out on its own while he drove around on his shift was delusional. Byrd left the property room, signed in, and walked through the quiet parking lot toward his cruiser. He slipped his baton out from a loop at his waist so he would not poke himself getting in the car.

A quick whistle came from the edge of the parking lot.

Byrd stopped in his tracks and looked over at Agent Curry in the dark. The agent stood in a navy or possibly black suit. The man was leaning with his backside on his bureau-issued sedan with the black paint of the vehicle shining in the meager light of the parking lot lamp.

The man stared over, and Byrd felt tension climb up the spine of his back.

"You waiting on someone?" Byrd asked.

No response. Byrd walked to his cruiser and stowed the baton on the front seat. He looked over the top of the car at the agent, who continued to stare unabated.

"Do you know what you're doing, Officer White?" Agent Curry asked.

"Starting my shift. You got a problem with that?"

Byrd hesitated a moment. He waited again for a reply, to no avail. He got in the cruiser, started the engine, and pulled out onto the street. He would loop over to reach Bridge Street. He meant to distance himself from both the station and the realization that he had somehow, most certainly, thrust himself out into the light.

CHAPTER NINETEEN

Byrd rubbed his hand on the back of his neck and watched as the same prison guard from his previous visits unlocked the door to the small room. "I need to take him with me tonight. You have something I can sign to release Ranney into my custody? You said on the phone that I didn't need a court order."

"Not for a limited release and for cause, no. Do you have something you can submit that's believable? That you can float with your superiors?"

"Yes. Ranney's mother died."

"So you're pulling him in the middle of the night."

"He's got a sister. A minor. We need to get her settled. Have Ranney sign some paperwork for guardianship until he's released."

"Let me bring him down. I haven't had a chance to pull him yet. Hang tight."

Byrd sat down in one of the chairs and grimaced. The room held an odor of sweat from its previous occupants. A nervous, anxiety-ridden spectrum of sweat. Byrd smelled the same odor in his cruiser some nights, mainly after an arrest when the perpetrators had time to rest in the back seat and realize what was on the horizon. It was the smell of fear and despair.

Byrd chose instead to wait just outside the room. He listened for footfalls in the hallway. He hooked his thumb in his waistband. He had checked his weapon on his way into the prison and felt naked without his sidearm. He leaned back on the doorjamb.

In twenty minutes, the men arrived. Michael brushed passed Byrd and entered the room.

"How long you need him?" the guard asked.

"I can have him back here in twenty-four hours," Byrd said.

"Make it eight. It will cause fewer raised eyebrows, and I can get him settled before my shift ends."

Michael sat in a chair.

Byrd entered the room and closed the door. "It's about time. You busy jerking yourself off?"

Michael tilted his head up, a smile threatening on his face. "Got myself a friend. I had nothing to do with it."

A single knock sounded, and the guard opened the door. He tossed Michael a heavy, sealed paper sack, which Michael set on the table and tore open. The street clothes he had worn into custody spilled out.

Michael looked up at Byrd as the guard closed the door. "I'm leaving here with you?"

"The Greek's request," Byrd said.

Michael unbutton his shirt. He slid his feet from his shoes. "Didn't know you were taking orders."

"I'm not. Now hurry up. We're on a clock, and we need to get back to Lowell."

"Hold your horses."

Byrd leaned back on the wall as Michael finished dressing. Thoughts raced in his head, and he needed answers. *Is Agent Curry truly a murderer?* He could not bring information to his bosses until he knew who was and who was not compromised. He was walking the edge of a deep chasm, with a haunting image in his head of a snake twisting, turning, and reaching to bite him in the ass. Each step, in aid to the Greek and the man before him, was another foot closer to the edge of that chasm. A drop ending in a landing of professional and personal doom.

Byrd pulled a set of handcuffs from his waist and motioned for

Michael to turn around. "We follow protocol until I got you on the road."

"No argument from me but get to it already."

Byrd cuffed Michael and took up the rear as the guard processed them out of the prison. Rain had ended, and the night was mild. But a crosswind blew, and a faint smell of static charge was in the air as if they were walking across the parking lot in an outer band of an approaching storm. Byrd got Michael settled in the back seat after removing the cuffs. He adjusted his gun snug at his hip and got into the driver's seat. The ride to Lowell was quick, and the two held off on talking until they reached the city.

$$\approx$$

Jimmy Tennyson appeared at the back door of the Skillet Bar as Byrd eased the cruiser down the alley.

Byrd set the vehicle in park and rolled down the window as Michael got out of the car. "I called someone earlier to get in and cover the rest of my shift. They should be on the road by now. I just need to return the wheels and clock out. You two tell the big man I'll be back in two shakes of a lamb's tail." He pointed to Jimmy and gestured to Michael with his thumb. "Make sure he goes nowhere until I get back, or there'll be hell to pay."

"You got my word," Jimmy said as he hiked up his jeans at the waist. "We're meeting upstairs. Office is too small. I'll leave the door unlocked but throw the bolt on your way up. And do me a favor. Change out of those threads. They make my palms itch."

Byrd looked at Jimmy, thinking he had a screw loose, and set the car in reverse. He eased back out of the alley.

$$\approx$$

Byrd walked up the stairs to the apartment after throwing the dead bolt home, as instructed. He quickened his step on hearing a commotion break out and a thunder of feet vibrate through the stairwell walls. He opened the door and beheld a fistfight between Michael Ranney and Tao Mann. Jimmy Tennyson stood to the side with a small smile playing on his lips. He cleaned under his fingernails with the blade of a Swiss Army knife, as if pretending the two in front of him held little interest. A woman dressed in a halter top and skin-tight white pants stood in the kitchen with her back to the room. She was putting together sandwiches of deli meats, lettuce, tomatoes, and slices of cheese. And Galen Stathakis sat facing the action with his arms crossed and resting on his stomach. A bottle of spirits sat behind him on the card table.

Tao put a headlock on Michael and pulled him down to the carpeted floor. Michael broke free of the hold, turned, and lay on his back with his forearms crossed, up and over his head. Tao straddled him and rained down punches.

"Isn't anyone going to do anything?" Byrd said to the room.

Galen's eyebrows rose. "They need to work it out between the two of them. Blow off some steam so we can have a calm, rational talk here."

Byrd got over to the two and wrapped his arms around Tao's upper arms from the back and lifted. But not before Tao got off one more swing that hit its target and bloodied Michael's lip. He might even have loosened a tooth or two. Byrd held Tao back as they stood looking down on Michael, who wiped his mouth with the hem of his T-shirt. Michael stood to take a seat at the table.

"Can I let you go? You going to sit down and keep your mitts to yourself?" Byrd said into Tao's ear.

Tao nodded as his breathing slowed and he relaxed his arms out of the hold. Byrd looked over at Jimmy and cocked his head toward the kitchen in query.

"That's Carol Anne. There was supposed to be a card game tonight," Jimmy said.

Galen leaned back in his chair. "Carol Anne. Can you go down and relieve Brendan? He jumped on the bar for Tao."

"Sure thing," she said. She gave a final rinse of two utensils in her hands. "Have at the food. I'll stop up later and pull together a few more sandwiches."

Byrd's eyes followed her as she walked out the door. He listened to her feet on the stairs and the sound of the door at the bottom of the staircase. "She single?"

Tao coughed. "Trust me—you don't want to go there. Swing by sometime, I'll hook you up with Sally James. She deserves a nice night out. And she won't be hanging on you like Spanish moss."

Byrd and Tao took seats and joined the others.

Galen tapped two fingers on the table. "Gentleman, we keep this discussion here between us. If this fed gets the idea that we're meeting about him, he's going to do something rash. We work this with as little disruption to the normal state of things as possible."

"What about the woman who just left?" Byrd said.

"She's square. Knows better than to ask questions. Or talk about what she may have seen or heard. Probably picks up more than we realize. But she's never let me down." Galen tapped his fingers once again. "Time to let us have it, Michael. The whole mess of it. What are we dealing with here? And before you start..." Galen lifted his chin in Byrd's direction. "You're the one that needs to prove something to me. What's said in here, what happens from here on out, we agree we're working together on this."

"I get it. We're good," Byrd said.

Galen continued, "What steps we take are not going to come back on us. Not now, and not some far-off day in the future. You're as exposed as we are."

Byrd nodded.

Galen drew his glasses down the bridge of his nose and turned his attention back to Michael. "Talk."

Michael dabbed again at his lip with his shirttail. "Goes back to that morning Jimmy stitched me up. My hip. I'd been up at the Chadwick School pulling copper." He looked in the eyes of each man at the table.

Galen cleared his throat as if to prompt Michael to continue.

He obliged. "I saw something big go down. I thought the best thing to do, keep everyone safe, was to stow myself back inside. I thought I was in the clear. I never thought I was seen." He adjusted his body on the chair. "I saw Curry. The fed. Saw him strangle that prick, Hamel, with a choke hold. Sergeant Ray Hamel."

Byrd rested his arms on the table and interrupted. "Agent Thomas Curry. He's working with the department here on reconnaissance for a federal gig."

"I was under the impression Hamel ate his gun," Galen said to Byrd.

"There's been no evidence I can find that proves otherwise. No tampering with the body. No clear signs the body was moved," Byrd said. "Nonetheless, I'm in the mind to believe Michael here."

Michael smiled. "Your guys didn't look hard enough."

Galen poured himself a drink. "Give me more on him," he said to Byrd.

"Basically, he's watching our vice operations. He's looking in on the SHARE program in the city. SHARE works at stopping drug use and addiction. Curry's been down in Woburn and Waltham as well. He's got the whole of Middlesex County."

Jimmy tapped Michael on the arm with the back of his hand. "If you weren't seen, how you on his radar?"

"Hold up. Think I can help with that," Byrd said. He grabbed the ouzo from in front of Galen and poured himself two quick shots with the bottle's cap. He passed the ouzo over to Jimmy's outstretched hand as he

SWEET, SWEET JAYNE

pointed to him. "When Michael gave me the nexus of this, I went through the log for the week of Ray's death. There was in fact a report of a break-in at Chadwick. Two men were dispatched there later in the week. They gathered evidence. Evidence that's now in the wind. A wrench was listed on the intake form. Prints were lifted, but the card is missing."

"I wore gloves," Michael said.

Jimmy closed the cap on the bottle after a shot and slid the ouzo back over to Galen. "You wipe down your tools before leaving them behind?"

Michael shook his head and pulled at the collar of his shirt. "No. And…" He pulled in a breath. He leaned back in his chair and turned his attention to the tray of sandwiches on the kitchen counter.

"And what?" Galen prompted.

"I kept having people walk off with my things. Or I'd leave them were I was staying. It was a real pain in the ass. So I scratched my initials in the wrench."

A moment of silence hit the room. A pause before Tao launched himself out of his chair and brought Michael to the floor once again.

"How could anyone be so stupid?" Tao said. He pinned Michael to the carpet with a forearm and elbow. He held up a palm to stop the others from interfering. "When this is over, and you've served your sentence, I want you to find someplace else. I don't care where. But I swear, if I see you again, I'm going to rip your face off and throw you off one of the bridges into the Merrimack. Conscious. So when you hit those big boulders under the water, you feel the full brunt of the impact."

"*Kátse kalá*," Galen said. He ran his open palm on the surface of the table as if clearing off dust. "What else is there, Michael?"

Michael shrugged.

"*Gamó to.*" Galen shook his head. "We need to work together here."

The two men slowly returned to their seats at the table. Michael ran his hand through his hair, from his forehead back. "I have something

161

the fed is looking for. On my way out of the school, I found a chain in the dirt. I figure it fell off as the guy was shoving Hamel into his trunk. It has a medallion on it with a date inscribed on the back."

Byrd leaned forward. "Medallion? Of Saint Michael?"

Michael nodded.

"How'd you know?" Galen asked, addressing Byrd.

Byrd relaxed his shoulders. "Saint Michael the Archangel. He's the patron saint of police officers. There was a photo of Ray in a box at his house. He's standing with his mother. Them posing at his induction ceremony. He has the chain around his neck in the picture." Byrd had one just like it given to him by his father. It hung from a nail by his phone in his kitchen. He would not risk losing it on patrol.

Tao sighed deeply, drawing everyone's attention. "Could explain why this guy is so pent-up on sending a message. A message you wouldn't have needed, Michael, if you just stood up to begin with. Instead of scurrying off to hide while your family pays."

Byrd interrupted. "I saw other pictures of Ray when I was at his house. You can see the chain at his neck. Michael, as a witness alone, isn't too threatening. He could easily be discredited. But him spinning a yarn and backing it up by physical evidence could be perceived as a real threat. A complaint would lead to Michael's description of the damage to the school in detail. It would put clearer eyes on the postmortem of Ray. And it would have people digging into whatever Agent Curry has his hands in."

"Could also explain why Michael's not dead," Tao said.

"There's that," Byrd said.

Galen dropped his chin and looked over the lenses in his glasses. "Michael, if you would've spoken to me and been honest with me, I wouldn't have Jayne working for me, out on the streets. Exposed. You asked that I 'keep an eye' on her."

"I didn't think the man had a clue I was there, Galen. How could I know he'd go after my family? I thought once I was back inside, it was as if it never happened," Michael said.

Galen reached over and pulled cigarettes from Michael's shirt pocket. The pack was compressed from Michael's tussles with Tao. Galen accepted a light from Jimmy and took a hit of his first cigarette in over a year. He pointed the two fingers cradling it at Byrd. "You bring Michael back tonight."

Byrd nodded. "As soon as we're done here," he said.

Galen took another deep drag of smoke into his lungs. Jimmy slid his lighter across the table to Galen, who kept his paw of a hand on the pack of cigarettes.

"Where're we at on this side of things?" Galen said.

"I have one of the *Maherákia* boys sitting on the hotel the feds put Curry up in. In Burlington. The room's clear, not a stitch out of place," Jimmy said.

"Where is he?"

"No sight of him yet," Jimmy replied.

Galen reached over and tamped out his cigarette. "I made calls. I have everyone's eyes open and ears to the ground. When he shows himself, I want you on him." Galen became distracted as Michael stood from the table and walked to the kitchen.

Michael grabbed a sandwich from the platter on the counter. He took a large bite of a ham and cheese.

"I'll be on the man," Jimmy said. "We can't do any sitting around and waiting."

Michael made noise behind them as he pulled a bag of potato chips down from a cabinet and a beer from the refrigerator. He returned to the table and realized, after a moment, that silence had descended. "What?"

Galen held his hand up off the table in a gesture to keep Tao in his seat. Galen turned his head to Jimmy. "What's your read on Officer

White here?"

Jimmy shrugged. He spoke as if the man himself was not seated beside him. "I say we get as much out of him as we can. Use him to help set up a negotiation, if needed. But I don't see him as a long-term ally. Whatever happens, he's still a cop. On the street, in this apartment, or in the bar. He's already picked sides by joining up with the boys."

Byrd shrugged, accepting the assessment.

Tao glared over at Michael as the boy went to town on a bag of Granite State potato chips. Tao sat forward in his chair. "Byrd went to see Michael when he called," he said. "He pulled me aside at the apartment. He's making the effort to work with us on this. I say we keep a close eye on everyone and accept his overtures." Tao pointed to Michael with his thumb. "Thanks to this chump, we need all the help we can get."

Galen lit up another cigarette and pulled the ashtray from the center of the table toward himself. "Agreed," he said, nodding once to Byrd. "Where's this neck chain, Michael?"

Michael wiped crumbs off the side of his face with the back of his wrist and finished chewing and swallowing the last bite of his sandwich. He took a moment to wash it down with a drink from his beer. "The apartment at O'Brien. In my old bedroom. Unscrew the fan and let it hang. It's in a clump of Silly Putty, tucked up into the ceiling."

Galen nodded and looked over at Jimmy. "First thing."

Jimmy stood from the table. "I need to visit our friends in town. I told them I would be by. Can you give them a shout?" he said.

Galen nodded.

"Do I want to know what friends?" Byrd asked.

The men ignored him.

"I got time for another ham and cheese?" Michael asked.

"Take it with you and get downstairs. Go say goodbye to your sister. She's sleeping on the couch in my office. You'll need to walk around front. The back door's locked," Galen said.

"All right if I take the beer from the refrigerator? I'll finish it in the car before Byrd drops me back."

"Get the hell out of here, will you?" Tao said.

Michael left the table. He grabbed the sandwich and the remainder of the six-pack at his own pace and clumped his way down the stairs.

"Does he even give a shit?" Tao asked.

"Some experience and exhibit grief differently," Jimmy said.

Tao rolled his eyes.

Galen sat back. A faint hint of a smile threatened. "He cares. He can't beat you at a physical fight, so he gets at you any way he can."

Tao stood from the table. "Where do you want me, Galen?"

"Work the bar. We need a central spot for communication, and you're it. It is all going through you. I want you confident and focused. Make decisions without doubt. I need to do some personal visiting. To make sure all avenues are open to us in neutralizing this threat." Galen poured more spirits in his glass.

Jimmy made his way to the apartment door before looking back over his shoulder. "This guy is neat and tidy. He's going to make a move soon."

Galen slipped the pack of cigarettes and the lighter into his breast pocket.

CHAPTER TWENTY

Jimmy Tens found Agent Curry with patience. He sat in his Duster for hours at the end of the Connector, sustaining himself on two pull-top cans of beer nuts and a gallon jug of water. He took a moment here and there to relieve himself in a nearby bush, eyes trained on cars exiting the off-ramp.

Curry's vehicle was easy to spot. His Plymouth was a Fury, and it was government-issue. A bare-bones model with no hubcaps and a heavy-duty cop suspension. Jimmy slipped into drive and slid up behind the car. It was a short drive to the station. Jimmy parked on the road where he had a good vantage point of traffic entering and leaving the lot. He slouched down in his seat and drummed the fingers of one hand on the top of his steering wheel.

≈

Byrd had returned Michael Ranney to the confines of Billerica with no difficulty. The guard commented that many would not even notice the inmate had taken a powder. Byrd relinquished custody and returned to Lowell for some sleep. He checked in with a short phone call to the Greek both in the morning and afternoon. He arrived for work the next evening in full uniform, entered the station at the side door, and signed in at the desk. He took the few minutes to stop to see if any notes were up on the board from the previous shift. He entered the guardroom and took notice of a contingent of men gathered in one corner. They were checking and rechecking their gear and speaking in serious tones.

Byrd sidled up to a fellow officer outside the group. "What's about to go down?"

"Raid on Elm Street. They were going to jump day after tomorrow, but Mr. FBI over there convinced them to get right on it. If he keeps swinging his dick around like a bat, he's going to get one of our guys hurt."

Byrd stepped out of the room. He would get on the road and out to the nearest pay phone to call down to the bar. He needed to let the Greek know that Agent Curry had made an appearance and they could now get a line on their man. He exited the building and pulled his cruiser to the end of the drive. Byrd turned to check traffic and spotted Jimmy Tennyson in a vehicle across the street. He locked eyes with Jimmy and pulled his cruiser up side to side, facing opposite directions so the two could talk.

Byrd cranked down his window. "He's in there, but he's about to head out on a raid with a few from the Narcotics Squad."

"Where're they headed?"

Byrd shook his head. "I'll follow with you after they're on scene. I don't want you getting in their way."

"I only care about eyes on the fed."

Byrd turned his head back to the station as two unmarked vehicles, a police cruiser and the wagon, pulled out from the lot. Agent Curry sat in the front seat of the lead car as it sped up and sailed through the red at the lights. Jimmy put his car in gear and looked over impatiently at Byrd, who took a moment before pulling forward. He reversed direction and followed. The men soon pulled up to a record store among a row of commercial buildings in the Back Central.

Byrd and Jimmy got out of their vehicles. They approached Manny Laczkó, who leaned against a beat-up VW Beetle among the row of cars on the street.

"Officer White. Hey, Jimmy," Manny said.

"What's happening?" Byrd asked.

"Contraband cigarettes. Whole roomful, not one tax stamp among the lot. And a small grow operation. Should be enough to charge with distribution."

Byrd nodded. "You didn't happen to see Agent Curry enter the building."

"The prick. He was third through the door."

The men waited in silence. The door to the right of the store opened, and three men were led out in handcuffs, heads down and walking with the resigned gait of the guilty. They were loaded into the back of the wagon as a couple of officers lingered on the sidewalk. Agent Curry walked out the door and casually strolled down the sidewalk.

"Where's he going?" Jimmy asked.

Manny shrugged and tilted his head toward the liquor store on the corner. "The packy?"

Byrd grabbed the sleeve of Jimmy's jacket as Jimmy stepped from the sidewalk. "It has to be me. You stay here," Byrd said.

"What you got going with the guy, Jimmy?" Manny asked.

Byrd answered before Jimmy could speak. "We need to talk to the man. A little harmless conversation."

"You better have it now, rather than later. Nixon's recalling a bunch of the guys from the field. With the president up for reelection and stories leaking like a sieve out of Washington, they're circling the wagons. Rumblings of misdeeds among the ranks. Don't think people care much, one way or the other, but whatever is going down is causing Dickie to pull his resources."

"I haven't been following the news," Byrd said.

Manny stood up straight, up off the car. "Whatever it is, I'll be glad when the prick down the street there hits the road. His air of superiority alone drives me nuts. And to think—what they must be paying the guy to stand by and watch all of us do the work. Nixon's saying drugs are 'public enemy number one.' Do they give us resources other than that dick looking over our shoulder, cramping our style? He told me I was to watch the line last run. The line, what line? Let him get down and dirty, roll with the guys. Live the life. Not just show up in a nice suit and spit-shined shoes."

Byrd stepped back a step and turned to Jimmy. "I'm serious. Stay here. I'll be back in ten."

The police wagon pulled out, and Byrd let it pass in front of him before crossing the street and heading down toward the liquor store. He reached the corner and found Curry leaning on the corner of the building.

"Something I can help you with, Officer White?"

Byrd motioned farther down, into the darkness of the alley. Curry stepped in with no hesitation.

"I hear through the grapevine that you're not long for the city," Byrd said.

"Word's come down."

"You wouldn't consider leaving things as they are, would you?" Byrd asked.

"I don't see your concern here, Officer White."

"Trying to have a direct, honest conversation with you."

"Direct, honest conversation? On ramblings you've listened to from a convicted felon? Are your staking your livelihood, your life, on stories from a jailhouse?"

"Did you just threaten me, sir?"

"Again, I'm confused as to what your concern is here, Officer White."

"The concern, sir. My concern is on limiting the damage."

"What's on offer?"

"Walk away. Unscathed. Ready to buckle down and get back to work in Washington. Nothing in your rearview, only scenery. Walk away and we call it a day."

"You make it sound so appealing and simple."

"It *is* simple. As simple as simple gets. I will personally guarantee you that Michael Ranney will not be a problem. I will not be a problem. And anyone else on the periphery will not be a problem once you leave Lowell. We'll turn over Saint Michael the Archangel. The written and physical evidence are already in your possession and their absence will remain a mystery and never brought to light. The death of Sergeant Ray Hamel and the death of Margaret Ranney will sit on the books as recorded. Those outside of our very tight circle will be none the wiser."

"Knew I'd have a problem with that goddamn thing around his neck. He had it on him at the school and got to the house and it was gone. Give me two days, Officer White. Two days to pull up stakes, square my assignment with the Boston office."

"Two days?"

"I'll call you at the bar, day after tomorrow. The bar with those new friends of yours who are on my ass. The tail, by the way, drops off now. You tell that derelict to find another hobby."

"Vietnam veteran."

"If I see him or any one of them, the girl, who I imagine is the one you're all trying to protect, is toast."

CHAPTER TWENTY-ONE

Galen Stathakis hung up the phone and made a note of a wager in his note-pad. He wrote in a shorthand he alone understood. He looked to the clock on the wall and noted the time. The mark cemented the call in his head and bolstered his near-perfect recall.

Jayne was out with Jimmy Tens, duckpin bowling for an afternoon. She would stay over in Dracut with Jimmy through the weekend, being the first Galen knew of to be formally introduced to and make acquaintance of Jimmy's old lady.

Jayne had been asking to return to school and threatened to put her foot down come Monday. Galen arranged assistance on numerous fronts, from having the janitor ready and willing to spirit Jayne away at the first sign of trouble. The man was a trusted ally and a retired marine, as well as a friend to the girl. Galen obtained the services of the school re-source officer to keep eyes and ears open to anomalies in the day-to-day. He enlisted a young man from a compatriot in Rhode Island to mirror Jayne's schedule and see her from classroom to classroom. The boy easily passed for a teenager and would be signed in as a transfer student thanks to an office administrator. The boy would not scare the other students and draw attention to Jayne, as the two closest to Galen would tend to do. The young man had arranged his own lodging at a boarding house in walking distance to downtown and would arrive Sunday evening.

Galen looked down the length of the room ahead of him. Sally James leaned on the bar by the taps as she spoke to Tao. She repeatedly tucked her hair behind her right ear in a nervous gesture Galen rarely noticed her exhibit before.

Tao lifted one shoulder in response to a question. He wiped his hands dry on a bar towel, a corner of which was tucked in a front pocket of his jeans. He glanced over to Galen and tapped the back of one of Sally's hands with his own. He stepped over to the end of the bar. "Sally's asking if we need help. Nights."

Galen nodded once and sat back on his stool. "Can you handle the phone for a bit?"

"Sure."

Galen tucked his notepad in his shirt pocket and stood. "Sally. Want to come back to my office?"

Sally drained the last inch of beer from her glass and followed behind Galen. He entered his office and sat in his chair. Sally chose the couch across from him, as opposed to the spare chair close and tight to his desk. He decided not to comment, because if she needed distance to ask her ask, he would give it to her.

"You have the floor. What can I do for you?" Galen asked.

Sally sat up straighter. "I was asking Tao if you need help here some nights. I've seen him work the bar alone when it's busy. I can make it easier. Serve the ones on the floor. Pull drafts, mix cocktails."

"I can't put you on," Galen said.

Sally sighed. "Why'd you ask me back here then?"

"I'm curious if you know why I can't hire you."

She looked down to the floor a moment then met Galen's eyes. "I can guess."

"Sally, how long you been walking the street?"

"Since I was seventeen."

"And it's my understanding—you're on your own. No one's running you."

"That's right. You can't make nothing if someone has his hand out every night. I keep my own schedule. Don't have someone stepping on me. Getting me to hustle when I'm beat."

"And when you first started out—they try to work you?"

"Hell, yeah. I wasn't two days on the corner, and I had some guy at me. For a while I took it indoors." She ran her hands down the top of both legs to her knees. "One of the best spots was the DMV, though, down on Plainview Avenue. Guys taking time out of their day. They're tired, stressed out. That place is hell. So I would hit them up in the parking lot on the way back to their cars. They needed relief." Sally pointed to herself. "Relief valve."

Galen smiled.

Sally followed suit. "They had an excuse to be away from home, away from work. It worked out for both of us."

Galen nodded.

"Eventually I made it back to the corner. More customers, faster turnaround. But I had a rough six months. One or two still wanted to own my ass. Broke my wrist, pulled my shoulder out of its socket. I got a few bruised ribs another night. This creep held his cigar to my thigh. Held me down until it burned through my jeans, down into my skin. Took the time to stoke it up while I hyperventilated."

"That was only the first six months," Galen said as a statement.

Sally nodded.

Galen rocked the chair back and forth a couple times. "You're a smart girl. Have you wondered why you've been left alone since then?"

She shrugged.

"Never crossed your mind?"

She looked up at the ceiling for a moment.

Galen leaned forward, leaning his forearms on the desk. "You started coming into my bar."

Sally's eyes widened a bit.

Galen sighed. "You've made the space your own. Using my bar as a place to unwind. A safe place. Which is all fine and good. I never officially sent word out to the street, but the ones causing you trouble knew the score. They knew that if you were hanging here, I may have something to say about you walking in here with a split lip. So they stepped back. They let you be." Galen leaned back in his chair. "Now ask me why I can't hire you."

"Why can't you hire me?"

"Because I can't be certain you're safe. Tao out there, Jimmy Tens, I know they can take care of themselves."

"And the girl you got running for you?"

"Leave Jayne out of this. She's finding her way, and I've got eyes on her."

"I heard about her mother. I'm sorry for her loss."

Galen shrugged and waved his hand dismissively. "We're talking about you. You—concern me, Sally. It's not the ones wanting to own your ass, as you say. It's the johns. The tricks. I can't guarantee the guys you're servicing are sane. And it only takes one."

Sally slid back in her seat on the couch.

Galen waited for her to respond. He gave her a moment and waited until her eyes settled back on his. "Do you want off the street?"

"I…" she said and blinked.

"You need to say it. Decide and own it. Do you want off the street?"

"One day. When I can find work."

"Not 'one day.' Do you want off the street, Sally?"

"Yes."

Galen leaned forward and smiled. He pulled the bridge of his glasses down and looked at her over the lenses. "You're done." He reached into his pants pocket and withdrew a fold of bills. He pulled some off and slid them across the desk under his palm. "Go home. Use this to cover you for a couple weeks."

Sally stood.

"Do some shopping. Get some clothes," Galen said.

Sally looked down at herself. She wore a long-sleeved knit that widened at the cuffs of the sleeves. No bra. A plaid skirt that would have been demure but reached only mid-thigh on standing.

Galen smiled. "Clothes you'd feel comfortable wearing to church."

"Gotcha," she said and picked up the money.

"I need the week to set you up. Be back here next Friday, and I'll have something for you. Until then, you hunker down. I won't mind seeing you in here, but the commerce ends."

"Thank you."

"This is your chance. Don't screw it up."

"I won't."

Sally walked out of his office.

Galen reached into his desk drawer for a thick phonebook. He paged through and found the number for the Rialto. It took only a short description to get his man on the phone. "James. I've got something for you. Monday morning after you drop Jayne, swing by Superior Court. Talk to whomever you can. Bailiffs, secretaries, maintenance guys. The guy who runs the coffee counter on the first floor. Everyone. And get whatever you can on Judge Brandt. Search out Brendan. Get more dirt from him. If the judge was up for arson, he's open to bending."

Jimmy agreed to be in Galen's office Monday afternoon with whatever he could gather. Galen hung up as Tao stepped in sight and leaned his shoulder on the doorjamb.

"Sally left here walking on air. Big smile on her face. You grant her three wishes or something?"

"Judge Brandt made the mistake of coming in here after Brendan. He showed us his hand. Let me know he's pliable like clay. I have Jimmy opening up the man's life. He'll be in here with the goods on Monday. Then a brief word with the good judge will be in order."

"You're great at those calls."

"Damn straight. We'll have him find Sally a job in the courthouse. Something challenging she can sink her teeth into, so she doesn't get bored. She has firsthand knowledge with lawyers and the court system. She might as well put that to use."

Galen swept his hand above his ear to the back of his head and tugged on his short curls. "Did you know she worked the Department of Motor Vehicles parking lot?"

Tao shook his head. "No. Great idea, though. Make that place a touch more human." Tao smiled and left the office to tend bar.

≈

Since her mother's death and over the course of a week, the reins had been pulled in and Jayne lost her independence. She discovered further that part of the increased tension amongst the group was because Michael had withheld information from Galen. Not smart on her brother's part. There were endless discussions in Galen's office to which she was not privy, and her exclusion caused additional stress.

Margaret's death had been ruled an overdose, the point of intentional or unintentional death being inconclusive. Either suicidal or accidental and, according to the men on high, no further investigation was warranted. The body was released after Jayne returned to school. She agreed with Galen to have Margaret cremated. And on an early evening, in front of a handful of people in attendance at the funeral home, a short prayer was intoned. She felt numb through it all. Michael was all she had left of her family.

≈

The following day, Galen arrived from the back hall of the Skillet and tossed his car keys to Jimmy Tens. "Take the Caddy. You can swing by in the morning to pick me up. I'll grab a ride home."

Jimmy hiked up his jeans and pocketed the keys. He turned his attention to Jayne. "You ready to hit the road?"

Jayne shrugged and grabbed the sweater she had set down on the bar. She had been staying most nights at Tao's house after her weekend in Dracut. Tao had gathered up her things at the apartment and stowed everything in the room he told her to consider her own. Her bicycle sat by the cases of beer in the bar's basement, unused and for the moment gathering dust. When she was back on her route, she would get deft at lifting it onto her shoulder and taking the stairs. The thought of riding it around the city once again had her dreaming of freedom.

Behind the bar, Tao nodded in Jimmy's direction. "Can you stay with her at the house when you get back? I should be home by nine."

"No problem," Jimmy said.

Jayne followed Jimmy out of the bar to Galen's Cadillac. He opened the long door wide for her to enter. The upholstery was soft velour, and she took little time in settling in.

"Where're we heading again?" Jayne asked.

"In town. A garage down near North Station."

"Boston?"

"It's not that far, kid. We'll be back before you know it. Besides, you don't want to be stuck back here. Bored out of your mind."

"If you say so. I've never been out of Lowell."

Jimmy smiled. "You're in for an adventure, then." He drove away from the curb and meandered his way out of the city. The shocks on the Caddy were exceptional. It was like floating down the road on clouds compared with the suspension on his beast of a car. He would take it slow and enjoy the ride.

Jayne toed off her shoes and set her stocking feet up on the dashboard. "No offense, but I feel like I'm being handed off. I can't get Galen to tell me when I can start running my route again."

"First. I want the company. I can avoid the strange looks at lights when I talk and sing to myself," he said and smiled. "Second. Galen will ease up on the Papa Bear routine. He's just an overly cautious guy and has fiercely protective instincts toward a certain teenager. I trust those instincts, and you should too."

"I know." She sighed and lifted a hair tie from the front pocket of her jeans. She bit down on it with her front teeth and ran her spread fingers through the long strands of her hair. She worked a quick braid before pulling her hair over her shoulder and securing the end.

"I want to get back to work. Start paying my own way."

"You will, cub."

≈

Jimmy drove down the slowly rising and falling route of the McGrath-O'Brien Highway, working the paper Tao had given him between two fingers. He sang along to "Waterloo Sunset" on the radio and glanced over at Jayne. She was staring at him with a quizzical expression as if commenting on his singing or choice of song.

Jimmy didn't care to know which. "Almost there," he said.

"What is this place? They going to work on Galen's car?"

"No. The garage is a front of sorts. These people are people we pay homage to. The action gets big enough, we pay a fee.

"Action from Lowell?"

"As far as their arm can reach. You stay small, you can fly under the radar. You hit a certain level, you come to an agreement. We drop a payment once a month to keep these guys from knocking on our door. Strange system—but it works. Until someone either gets too greedy or there's a misunderstanding, which is common in our world."

"What does Galen get from them in return?"

"Peace. And freedom to conduct his business as he sees fit."

Jayne looked out the passenger window as they passed by the Museum of Science. The sunlight shimmered off the waters of the Charles River.

Jimmy drove on, having no qualms about tailgating the car ahead of them. "This will only take ten minutes, tops. You can get out and stretch your legs but stay by the car. Honk the horn if you need me. We'll stop in the North End after for some cannoli." He drove by North Station and the Garden. He parked at an unmetered spot near the front of the garage. He exited the car, hiked up his jeans, and walked to the entrance, an open overhead door.

Two men made their way out, each with a beer in their hand. One of the men was a low-level earner with two large-gap teeth at the front of his wide mouth. He stood in a relaxed way as if to project an air of confidence. He failed. The other man had thirty years on him. He was the owner of a club in Southie and looked the part. He wore his pants high on his round waist, with no belt. A shiny metal money clip poked out from a pocket.

The fat man belched and pointed his can toward Jimmy's car. "You have a kid I don't know about?"

"She's family, yeah. No worries." Jimmy looked over his shoulder at Jayne as she leaned on the side of the car.

She glanced around, more interested in the subway passing on the tracks above their heads than the men who came out to greet them. She was in the sun, but not far from the shade and shadows cast by the overhead rail. Its path traveled in front of North Station and curved up toward the markets of Faneuil Hall and the many steps surrounding Government Center.

Personally, Jimmy missed Scollay Square, his father's old stomping ground, a piece of Boston that thrived through the First and Second World Wars. A piece of the city that grew sullied and withered as the years moved into the postwar era. A death knell sounded, and in 1962 it all came tumbling down. The metropolitan area, in one fell swoop, lost its character and draw. Its demise was spurred on by those in power. Simple pleasures like hot dogs from Joe & Nemo existed no more. Childhood memories Jimmy held dear from before his family moved out from Boston. He would never experience the life his father drew out of that time and place.

Jimmy gave Jayne a reassuring smile and walked farther into the garage. He took a seat on a chair near the rear of the garage. The other two sat down on a long wooden bench by a small desk.

The young man with the gap teeth offered Jimmy a lit joint. "You or your daughter want a beer?"

"No, thanks. Not staying long," Jimmy said, accepting the smoke. The herb made two rotations before the side door opened and Kevin arrived. The man he came to see. Jimmy passed over the scrap of paper from Tao. "This is the guy we need a line on. He's FBI, in the field in Lowell. But he's got to be reporting in here."

"Boston office is right up the road," Kevin said. "We'll ask around, find out if his name pops up in our circles or is bandied about on the street."

"You got anyone in the BPD that can go snake their way into headquarters?" Jimmy asked.

"Wouldn't tell you if we did. That's not information we'd share. I told you we'll ask around, and that's what we'll do."

Jimmy nodded. "Where's the boss today?"

The question was met with a shrug, and Kevin pulled a black bag from under the desk and opened the zipper as Jimmy leaned back. From their spot in the garage there was a sightline to the street, but they were deep enough in the garage and positioned in a way to keep their business private.

Kevin pulled out a small, dirty-white towel and laid it out on the desk. He pulled three guns out of the bag and checked each in turn. They were a Beretta 950, a Colt Commander, and a FB P-64. Kevin confirmed they were unloaded and handed the first over for inspection. "I can get something different if these don't do it for you," he said.

Jimmy held and examined each weapon. He waved off the joint before it was extinguished. He tested the weight of each gun, the feel, slide action, and resistance on the trigger. "This one here. The CZAK," Jimmy said, pointing at the FB P-64. "With some adjustments."

"Adjustments?" Kevin asked.

"A better grip. One that's not going to slip. And file off that finger guard."

The expression Jimmy met on lifting his head was of indignation.

"For the grip, you can slap on electrical tape. The guard is plastic. I don't see you having a problem taking care of these issues yourself," Kevin said.

Jimmy looked back down at the gun. He picked it up in the palm of his hand and ran the pad of his index finger over the frame. "I can feel the serial number. It's like reading braille. What did you guys use, a nail file?"

Kevin grabbed the gun from under Jimmy's perusal. "We'll hit it with some acid. Give me a couple days."

"I've got backup," Jimmy said. He reached in his pocket for a wad of cash held together by two rubber bands. "Can you do better on time?"

"You throw me extra, I'll have Bugs Bunny here hand-deliver it day after tomorrow."

"Nope. Give Tao a call and I'll swing by to pick it up."

Kevin rolled his eyes. "Just meet me in Sully's, day after tomorrow. Same time."

"Same Bat-channel," the kid said.

Kevin slapped the side of the young man's head, hard, with an open palm. "Shut up. Did I tell you to talk?"

≈

Jimmy made his way out of the garage and walked around the hood of the car. "Ready to hit the road?"

Jayne opened the passenger door. "Sure thing, Dad."

"Smart-ass."

She got in, and Jimmy eased the car into the road, checking the street for oncoming traffic.

As they walked the narrow streets of the North End, high winds whipped strands of Jayne's hair out of its tie. She was happy. Jimmy held out another in a series of cannoli for her to devour as they headed back to the car. She cradled it in a napkin and took another cautious bite, careful to keep the delicate pastry from breaking apart in her hands.

CHAPTER TWENTY-TWO

Jayne yawned as they neared Lowell. Jimmy let up on the gas and braked as he exited the Connector to Thorndike Street. He eased through the yield and spied a police cruiser as it pulled out of Central Street. The vehicle accelerated and sat on his rear bumper as he approached the lights ahead. He divided his sight between the road and the tail behind as Jayne sat with her head back and eyes closed. She was unaware of the shift.

They drove by the YMCA, the train station, and South Common. They passed under the Lord Overpass and the sound of the two-beat staccato police horn sounded. Blue and white lights reflected off the Caddy's mirrors. Jimmy waited until he was up from under Middlesex Street before he slowly pulled over to the side of the road. He patted Jayne's leg and took a mental inventory in his head.

He was good. The gun he carried under his arm was licensed under the 1968 Massachusetts statute 131, allowing him to carry the registered handgun outside his residence. Jimmy breathed deep and kept his eyes on his mirrors.

From the patrol car, two officers approached on either side. The exchange began with a demand for Jimmy and Jayne to exit the vehicle, instead of the expected request of license and registration.

"May I ask why you pulled me over?" Jimmy asked.

"Get out of the vehicle and walk to the rear."

Jimmy looked over and nodded to Jayne. She pulled her bag up from the floor and over her head. The strap came to rest on her shoulder and across her chest. They exited the car, and Jimmy stepped to the rear. As he reached the trunk, he was spun around forcefully, and the officer searched him. He drew out the gun from Jimmy's holster under his army jacket. He handed the weapon to his partner, who checked the safety and tucked the gun in his own waistband at his back.

"I have a license for that. It's in my wallet," Jimmy said.

The hands returned, pushing Jimmy's torso down on the trunk and pulling his wallet from his back pocket. The officer looked down at the license photo. "James Samuel Tennyson. Just the guy we're looking for."

A handcuff was clicked shut on Jimmy's right wrist, and his left arm was drawn back violently to meet at his back.

"What's the charge?" Jimmy asked.

"I'll read you the warrant when I read you your rights in the car."

"You have nothing on me. I have a right to know the charge." Jimmy watched as the second officer left Jayne to go over to the passenger side of the Cadillac.

The officer reached in and snagged the keys from the ignition. The action and its ramification hit Jimmy like the swell of a wave crashing to shore.

Jimmy whipped his head around and met Jayne's eyes. "We taking her with us?" Jimmy asked, his eyes never wavering from Jayne's. "She's a minor. She can't just be left here. Take us both, so she can make a call and have someone pick her up."

"We ain't no taxi service." The officer placed a hand on Jimmy's shoulder and brought him up to a standing position. Jimmy swung an elbow back, using the momentum of his body to clock the man in the mouth.

The other officer grabbed Jayne's arm and pulled her away from the commotion. "Stop," he said. "Stop. Or I'll say she ran out into traffic."

Jimmy turned.

The man tugged Jayne over closer to his body. "You don't want anything to happen out here, do you? Get in the back. With no trouble. And we'll leave the young lady to her own devices."

Jimmy allowed them to wrestle him into the back seat of the police cruiser. He called out to Jayne in the process. "Get across the street to Furey's, Jayne. Get off the street—run!"

≈

Jayne crossed the lanes of traffic and looked back to watch the cruiser pull around the Cadillac and out into the road. She ran down the sidewalk to the corner of the brick front of Furey's Cafe. A car screeched to a stop beside her, causing Jayne to trip on a crack in the concrete.

"Jayne Ranney?" a voice asked.

Jayne turned cautiously and reached her hand into her bag.

"Miss Ranney?" The man stepped out of his car and onto the sidewalk. "I'm Agent Curry with the FBI. I've been instructed to bring you in. To protective custody."

She looked both ways on the street and watched a few cars pass in front of them.

Agent Curry pulled the badge from his coat pocket and flipped open the cover. "In my job, it's all about procedure, Miss Ranney. I'm afraid I need to follow my orders and get you off the street. Into the protective arms of the US government."

Jayne backed up a step. "Let me just go inside. Get someone to let me call home."

Agent Curry chuckled low. He grabbed her arm and turned her to the wall to outfit her with his own set of cuffs.

"Hey," she said.

After securing her wrists, Agent Curry tugged Jayne over to the edge of the sidewalk. He opened the door of his car, pushed her head down, and shoved her into the back seat. He walked around the rear of the vehicle, his eye trained on Jayne as she struggled to sit up in the back seat. When he reached the driver's-side door, he looked over at the bar. As expected, no one was watching from the small, high windows on either side of the door. The commotion did not merit an investigation by those nursing drinks within the dark tavern. Curry put the car in drive and swung out into Fletcher Street traffic. "Lay down on the seat and keep your mouth shut."

"Who are you?"

"Your keeper. You'll be fine if you stay down, stay quiet, and listen to what I tell you."

Jayne felt trapped and in immediate danger. She trusted the fear that rose as a sensation of heat on her body. She laid back, and the handcuffs cut into her wrists from her weight. Regardless, she raised her legs and pulled her knees up into her chest. She struck the door with her feet. She pulled them back again, into her chest. She aimed higher this time, to strike out for the window.

Agent Curry turned in the front seat and hit an immediate, glancing blow to Jayne's head with the butt of his service revolver, incapacitating her.

She soon regained consciousness, in severe pain, little strength to sit upright, and in a spreading dampness of urine that released as she traveled a current of overriding fear.

The blow worked in the man's favor. It made Jayne docile and easy to transport.

CHAPTER TWENTY-THREE

At the Skillet, Tao amused himself by listening to the discussions around him as he poured 7 and 7s. Two women broke into fits of laughter at one of Brendan McHugh's many overused jokes. Tao rinsed out a pour spout in the sink and opened a new bottle of Seagram's.

The front door to the bar opened with force and Officer White entered. He walked over to stand across from Tao at the taps. He threw out a thumb as if hitchhiking on the side of the road, and the two moved to the back hallway.

"Jimmy Tennyson is at the station," Byrd began.

"For what?" Tao asked.

Byrd slowly shook his head. "I'm not totally clear on that. And not the issue. I was coming on shift, and he's there. Toody and Muldoon grabbed him up and left Margaret Ranney's daughter with the car on the side of Thorndike Street. I drove by on my way here and no sign of the girl. City impound is hooking up the tow now."

"Why didn't Jimmy make his call?"

"Not until he's booked. I couldn't get a word out of the guys. They're sitting on him. If he's not charged, they don't have to let him use the phone."

Tao left his side and moved back into the room. "Sorry, folks. Locking up early. I need all of you gone."

A few groans were emitted in response, but all six patrons prepared to leave.

Brendan stood from his stool. He braced his hands on the lip of the bar. "Tell me what I can do."

Tao nodded slowly. "Get down to the police station. Ask for Jimmy at the desk. His last name is Tennyson. Sit there until he's released. Make noise if you have to. Bring him straight back here. And don't be grilling him."

"He wouldn't say nothing to me anyway," Brendan said.

Tao walked to the telephone and called Galen, who was dropped home in the last hour. Tao spoke with little inflection of the fear he felt and ended the call. "So—you working right now?"

"You can come for a ride-along. We're looking for a missing person, after all."

Tao pulled a set of keys from his pocket and Brendan exited before Tao locked the door. The place was cleared within minutes.

≈

Tao turned off the light to the bar sign to signal that the bar was closed. He took a moment to secure Galen's office. He and Byrd made their way out the back and up the side alley at a jog. Once on the sidewalk, they approached the running cruiser sitting at the curb.

Tao caught Byrd's attention over the roof of the car. "Galen's on his way down. Where do we start?"

"Back to Thorndike Street and we'll double back. We'll swing by the Ranney apartment. Check to see if anyone hanging on the Common has seen her."

Tao drummed fingers on the roof. "The kid would have made it here by now. Called, at least."

"You're right to worry," Byrd said and nodded. He pulled open his door at the same time as Tao, and they both slid into the car. Byrd set the car in drive and pulled away from the curb. "I'd rather not call attention, if it's at all possible. I'd like to bring more people in on this, but I don't know who to trust."

Tao watched the sidewalks and side streets as Byrd drove farther down the road. They took a right at the gas station and drove down Thorndike. The Cadillac was gone, and there was no sign of Jayne. When they reached O'Brien Terrace, Byrd drove a hundred feet up over the sidewalk onto grass and over a pedestrian way to reach a spot in front of the apartment. He easily gained access to the premises with a tool he pulled from his back pocket and held the door for Tao.

After a quick search and a swing by the Common, Byrd dropped Tao at the Skillet. He drove back to the station and gave a quiet word to Danny, notice that he may be off radio and to arrange coverage. He also took the time to satisfy his curiosity by reading the log of the two who picked up Jimmy Tennyson. If the notes were any indication, they were parked at the end of the off-ramp from the Connector for nearly two hours. A call at a house on Gorham Street went unanswered until a second unit intercepted the call and responded. The infraction was clear enough to support a reprimand.

CHAPTER TWENTY-FOUR

The ride was short. The sky darkened, and a light rain began to fall. The car entered a heavily wooded area, and Jayne Ranney raised her head to sneak a peek out of the very bottom of the side window. She looked one way and turned her head, pushing up on her side, to see the other side of the road. Gravestones, as far as the eye could see. Gravestones of Lowell Cemetery.

Jayne lay back down on the seat, and the bump on her head throbbed with pain. She could feel her hair was slick with blood. A pull of exhaustion began to affect her mind and her body. The threat still existed, driving the car in silence, but after the immediate attack, her senses were taking a break, and she could not muster the strength to scream or protest her abduction.

The car hit a pothole, and Jayne let out a groan. The handcuffs dug into her wrists as she tried to pull her arms forward to prevent a fall to the floor. Curry slowed the vehicle and turned onto another narrow road in the cemetery. He drove over a slow rise to a small stone building that appeared too large to be a mausoleum. He pulled up and over the grass to park to the side of the structure. There was no light on the building, and the branches of a tall sycamore hid the car from the road of travel. The agent turned off the engine and turned in his seat.

Jayne was startled as he reached over and down for her arm.

"Steady," he said sternly. His other hand came around with his keys, and he unlocked the handcuffs. "We need to walk. You speak a word, make a sound—I shoot you in the head. Nod if you understand."

Jayne nodded. She sat up slowly and placed her left hand on her right wrist, attempting to ease the pain.

Curry tucked his keys in his pocket. "We're getting out. You run—I shoot you in the head. Nod if you understand."

Jayne nodded.

Curry thumbed a switch by the dome light. He opened his door, and Jayne sat in the dark as he got out and opened the rear door to reach for her. She let him lead her and stood on her own outside the car as he adjusted his gun in the holder under his suit coat. Jayne swayed on her feet, mildly nauseous and dizzy.

Curry gestured across the graves to a line of trees in the distance. She started forward, but she was unsteady on her feet. She made small, determined steps to stay upright. Curry grabbed her by the back of the neck and quickened their pace between stones and over gradations. They came to the border, and he helped her over the short stone wall that ran down the edge to the street. They made their way through the trees, over pine needles spread at their feet like carpet. The rain picked up but did not reach them in full force because of the cover of leaves over their heads.

Curry grabbed again for Jayne's neck, which helped her to stay upright. She strained to see her way over stones and fallen branches. They came up behind a brown house with a large vegetable garden past its seasonal prime. A couple of broken, rotting pumpkins littered one full lane of soil.

The agent steered Jayne up a set of wooden back stairs and off to the side by a large empty flowerpot. Curry turned the knob on the door, but it was locked. He reached in his suit coat to an inner pocket and extracted a small leather pouch. He released a zipper and pulled out a thin tool. He leaned over and had the door open in seconds. He grabbed for Jayne's arm and steered her through the door ahead of them.

Across the room stepped a man with an Afro of dark hair and bushy sideburns warming his jaw. He leaned on the entrance to the kitchen in a long bathrobe over jeans and a white T-shirt. The hairs on his toes stood out on the pale white skin of his feet. He pointed an index finger at them while holding a coffee cup in the same hand. "I distinctly remember locking that door."

Jayne stepped beside the table, as prompted by a short push from her captor.

Curry pulled his suit jacket aside and revealed the butt of his gun, along with a small, simple federal badge at his belt. "Do you recognize me, Mr. Donato?"

Mr. Donato nodded once and glanced at Jayne before turning his attention back to Agent Curry. "You're the fed that was in the SHARE offices a couple times six months ago. Sat in on a session I was in."

"That's right," Curry said. He kept his hand on his hip and his gun exposed. "You mind if we all step in the other room? Get comfortable and have a discussion?"

"This some kind of raid or something? Because I got nothing."

"Don't you think I'd have more with me than a girl barely out of pigtails if I was going to breach the premises to conduct a search?"

Donato shrugged and took a sip of the drink in his cup. He turned to leave the room, and Jayne and Curry followed. They stood on a large oriental rug that was in desperate need of a cleaning. Crumbs and debris littered the floor. Donato sat in an easy chair and set his cup down on a small table.

Curry pushed on Jayne's elbow in the direction of the couch.

Heat rose on her face from immediate feelings of discomfort and shame. "I can't," she said. She ran her hands down from her hips, down her outer thighs.

Both men looked to the apex of her legs. To the stain, darker than the drops of rain that had landed on her outer clothes.

"Jesus," Donato said.

Curry pointed with a thumb to the wall by the hallway. "Stand over there."

She stepped around the edge of the couch and a floor lamp. She stood by the wall as instructed, within Curry's line of sight.

The agent stayed on his feet and let his suit coat fall back into place. "You are John Adam Donato. A.K.A. John Doe. You live in this house on Deerfield Street alone. You recently completed a federally funded drug rehabilitation program. And you are working your way to being a productive member of society. A man who pays his taxes. Taxes that pay into the very program that assisted you in weening off a Class A narcotic."

"Okay," John said suspiciously.

"You are also the man who procures and distributes at least 80 percent of the heroin product in the city of Lowell."

John reached for his cup and took a sip of his coffee, as if trying to project calm.

Curry crossed his arms over his chest. "Let me lay it out. How I see it. You try the drug for the first time, and it's love at first sight. You begin a committed relationship with it. You sail through time in a perpetual daze. And it hits you one night. Maybe you mix in a bit of cocaine and are speed-balling right to an epiphany. Like in the cartoons, and a light bulb appears over Mr. Peabody's head. You look around. You see your friends sprawled out on sofas, on the floor. People around you strung out to the gills. And you think, man, if I get straight, I can make a killing off this stuff."

John Doe set his cup back down.

Curry's eyebrows rose. "How am I doing so far?"

John shrugged.

Curry nodded and continued his theorizing. "You learned from the mistakes of your predecessor. A woman, I believe, which is most unusual. You get clean. You never cut or manage the product here, where you live. You spread it around to a few apartments in the city. So if one goes down, you carry on as if nothing has happened. Only thing I'm curious about, though. Where do you keep all the money you're raking in? You're obviously not living high on the hog. Where are you socking it away for another rainy day?"

John Donato sat forward and set his forearms on his thighs. "You know so much—why you here? Why not just demand a cut of the action like you do with my dealers? I got no problems with coming to an agreement. But why we talking in front of the kid over there?"

"Jayne. My name is Jayne Ranney," she said.

Curry turned his head and met Jayne's eyes with a sharp expression. One that threatened further violence.

"You related to Michael Ranney?" John asked.

Jayne nodded.

Curry put his hands on his hips and lifted his chin to John. "Was he selling for you?"

"Only weed. Here and there. Michael didn't want anything to do with horse. He crashed here sometimes. But he stayed out of my business. What're you doing—with his sister, I assume?"

"I'm presently in a silent negotiation, and she's my collateral. I need a place to keep her for a few days. A place that will free me up to get things done. Figure this is as good a place as any." Curry stepped back a step and sat on the couch. "First, I need you to tell me all of it, so I'm confident I can count on you to protect my interests."

"You already seem to know everything. How is that, by the way?"

Curry shrugged. "I'm great with people. I negotiate like a master. You go away on a federal rap, it's serious business. Business you cannot come back from. Even on the street, they talk. And I listen to it all."

"So what's there left to know?"

"The money."

John sighed. "What about it?"

"You're not making regular, nightly drops of deposits to a bank. So where you stashing the greenbacks? You wisely caught on not to operate where you live. I assume there are no ill-gotten bills to be found here in the house."

"How do I know you won't clean me out? Run away with all my hard earnings?"

"The information, the location you give me tonight is insurance only. Right now, I mean to settle the one loose thread I have hanging and leave the state. Simple as that. But I need you to divulge the information to me now, so I'm not tempted to just end this discussion here with a bullet in your brain."

John shook his head in defeat. "My father's house. Estranged father, I should say. Never had much contact with him. But when kids were practicing tuck-and-cover drills at school, my father was out digging a fallout shelter in the backyard. He never lived with us, but Mom talked him up. About how eccentric he was and how it was a sign of intelligence. Where personally, I think he toes the line of madness like his folks before him." John let out a short chuckle before continuing. "He built this big-ass shed in his yard to cover the hole in the ground. My mom said he was paranoid. Afraid that when the big one fell, there'd be a rush of people on his place. So, he dug at night and told anyone that got too close and was curious that he was working on the septic. And now it sits all forgotten. That damn, sad sight of a shed collapsing on top of it. My father probably forgot about the damn thing. So I found my way in one night when I was a teenager. More out of curiosity than anything else. And farther down the road, when I needed it, that light bulb in my head you spoke of lit up."

"Where's the bath?" Curry said.

"What?"

"Bathroom. For the girl."

John stood. "Upstairs."

Curry nodded and stood himself. He steered Jayne, by a hand to her lower back, down the hall and to the base of the stairs. She climbed with the two men following close on her heels. Curry stepped around her at the top of the stairs. He flipped a switch to turn on the light of the bathroom across the hallway. He entered and pulled the curtain back to start the hot water.

"Strip," Curry said.

Jayne looked over her shoulder at John and back at Curry. She shook her head.

Curry glanced once around the room and stepped out into the hall. "Don't lock the door," he said.

"Or you'll shoot me in the head?" Jayne replied.

Curry shut the door and turned to John. "You have any other interior rooms?"

John shrugged. "They're all interior rooms, aren't they?"

"No windows, no doors to the outside."

John shrugged again.

Curry sighed and glanced down the hall. "I need a hammer, nails, and a couple loose boards. You have another john, John?"

"Off the kitchen."

Curry shrugged his suit coat off his shoulders and laid it over the hallway rail. "Go get me the tools."

≈

Jayne eased down to sit on the side of the tub. She peeled off her jeans and took off her other clothing. She took her shower, savoring a few extra minutes at the end, under the spray of hot water after cleaning herself, her eyes closed, her hands and arms limp by her sides. The door opened, and a draft made its way around the curtain. She turned off the water and reached for the towel hanging from a rod on the wall. She wiped herself down hastily and carefully put the towel to her head. She dabbed at the raised wound and pulled the cloth away to look at the red stain. She discovered that the bleeding had lessened to an extent. She patted dry her hair and worked more vigorously on the long strands.

Jayne listened to a clatter by the sink and wrapped the towel around herself before opening the curtain. Curry stood in the room. The sleeves of his white dress shirt were rolled up to his elbows. He was emptying out the contents of the medicine cabinet. Jayne stared and slowly stepped from the tub as he knelt with one knee and cleared out below the vanity.

Jayne tucked the corner of the towel in more securely above her chest. She stepped back and sat on the lip of the tub.

Curry turned his head to look out the open door of the bathroom. John appeared at the top of the stairs holding two dirty two-by-fours as a hammer listed from the pocket of his bathrobe. He set them down at his feet .

"Where've you been?" Curry said.

"I had to run out to the shed." John dusted off his hands and walked down the hallway.

Jayne put her hand across her chest, on the towel. "You're not really leaving me in here, are you?"

Curry stood and emptied all the items he collected into a small trash bin, including a can of abrasive and a dusty box of mothballs.

John returned and handed Jayne a stack of clothes—a sweater, undershirt, and a pair of pants. They were large, likely to fit John, but she was grateful. She closed the lid of the toilet and set them down.

"Get me another bin," Curry said.

"Bin?" John asked.

"Trash can."

John returned. Curry loaded up the remaining items from the vanity and Jayne's soiled clothes, tissues, and used Q-tips from up off the floor. He pushed the can to the door, but John had disappeared. The man returned a moment later with a large blanket and a pillow. He dropped them by Jayne's feet and lifted the trash out the door.

"Can you at least tell me why me?" she said to Curry as he walked over the threshold.

He paused only a moment. "You flood this room, and we are the only ones that will respond. We'll stuff you in the smallest closet in this house or nail you into a box."

Curry pushed the sleeves of his shirt down and buttoned the cuffs. He reached out and closed the door, leaving her question unanswered. Jayne reached for the clothes and lifted up the sweater to reveal a pair of thick, heavy wool socks. She sighed and felt a moment of relief, a moment of hope. The big, curious-looking man with hairy toes had a heart.

At the contact of hammer on nail outside the door, Jayne's head came up in a snap. Across from her, she watched as her book bag vibrated and swung from a hook in a short pattern to match the strikes. She smiled weakly, thankful for the two Hershey bars Tao had tucked in the bag the day before.

CHAPTER TWENTY-FIVE

Michael Ranney spotted the danger at the bottom of the back stairs but was too late to slow up or reverse direction on his ascent. To do so would only delay an attack. Or worse, back him into a corner once he cleared the landing and reached the locked door. The inmate below stood tall and appeared willing and able to pursue Michael either way. The intimidating man had arrived at the prison within the past week. He carried himself as if he bore the weight of a large chip on his shoulder. He was a loner who didn't speak to other inmates or pair off as the men usually did. Some ran into old acquaintances and used the first week to catch up, spread news of the neighborhood.

No. He wasn't settling in at all. And his eyes beaded in on Michael as Michael got closer to the base of the stairs. Michael reached the floor and caught sight of a second man who was leaning on the wall under the steps. He was smaller in stature but had the same intense stare and focus.

Each day the door to Michael's cell opened, he was primed for trouble. He made sure to be on edge, to be prepared, especially since he returned from Lowell. Unfortunately, he feared he was not up to the challenge of defending himself against the two men. The larger grabbed Michael's arms and turned him to the side so his back was to the man under the stairs. Michael pulled back but could not break free from the hold. He craned his head around and received a haymaker to the stomach in return. The hit doubled him over, and he sank down to his knees. Lengths of cloth, likely ripped from a standard-issue bedsheet, were swung over his head from behind, and Michael's hands came up to pull at the strips of a garrote. The material was pulled tight and cut off his air as he struggled to breathe.

The assailant behind was down on one knee and set his other knee at Michael's back as he pulled the ligature tighter. The large man in front of Michael smiled. It was a slow, satisfied type of smile. The one Michael imagined the man wore sitting back after a meal of prime rib and potatoes, the meat having been cooked to perfection.

Michael swung his elbow back. He attempted to twist to the side, but it was useless. He could not find purchase or relief. He struggled desperately with a determination to wipe off the self-satisfied smile from the one in front.

In moments, he began to experience telltale signs of the end, a line to unconsciousness like a slow steam engine train traveling into a tunnel. His arms fell at his sides as strength left his body. His sight began to grow dim and narrow as he looked down the hallway. Away from the eyes of the imposing man. Down to witness Roy walk up the corridor in a relaxed, slow manner. The sight of him in Michael's last moments caused Michael a deep pain to his heart as his sluggish pulse slowed. Before his eyes closed for the last time, he glimpsed a shine of silver in Roy's right hand.

Roy weighed 130 pounds wet, so there were marked differences in stature to the standing man. Roy stepped up, lifted his arm, and surprised the big man only a second before stabbing out for a vulnerable spot below the armpit. The smile on the man died, and the strength of the garrote loosened on Michael's neck when the big man fell to his hands and knees in front of them. The man clawed at the gushing wound. He fell to his side and blood flowed, pooling out from under his body.

Roy wore his own smile, one Michael strained to capture. He met Roy's eyes, and the boy nodded before stepping around and slashing wide at the man at Michael's back. The attacker lifted his arms to protect himself, abandoning the hold on Michael's neck. The speed and efficiency of

Roy's moves appeared practiced, skill that was executed with unwavering confidence.

Michael struggled to catch his breath as Roy went at the other man. Roy slashed at the tendon on the man's ankle as he tried to stand. He brought him to the floor once again. The man, in a last-ditch effort to escape his fate, grabbed for the rail of the stairs and lifted himself to his feet. Roy dispatched him as well, this time with a stab to the stomach. The man stared into Roy's eyes as if in a final plea for leniency. Roy turned the knife and moved the blade north.

Roy wiped his hands on the man's shirt once he fell, close enough to the wound to know the act would soon be covered in additional blood. He grabbed the hem of the shirt and pulled at an edge of masking tape on the hilt of the blade and unwound a long strand, careful to keep his fingers from touching the weapon. He dropped the knife at his feet. Roy stepped over to Michael and threw Michael's arm around his shoulder. He lifted him with effort, and the two moved down the hall at a quick pace. They eased their stride at the end of the hallway. They turned the corner and walked the main corridor to the entrance to the common area.

Michael began to walk under his own power. The two crossed the room at a normal pace and climbed another set of stairs. They made their way down to Michael's cell. Michael collapsed back on his bunk. Roy washed his hands briskly in the basin and sat down beside him on the bed. He patted Michael's knee.

"How did you just appear like that?" Michael said. "It was as if I called out to you."

Roy shrugged.

"Who are you?" Michael asked.

Roy stood and leaned an arm on the top bunk as he looked down on Michael sitting on the bed. "My boss and the Greek have an agreement. A barter system of sorts. This time it was the Greek's turn to ask. And there may be some money involved to compensate my time off the streets."

"Your boss. From where?"

"New York."

"Why didn't you just tell me? What was all that green to the gills playacting? The black eye?"

Roy shrugged again and stood tall. "That bastard gets a visit from me on my way out. The only way I could manage the protection was to be who I was. Who I was to you."

"Who you were to me. And you're saying what, exactly?"

Roy sighed.

"I get it," Michael said.

"No. You don't. I've been with men and women. I've played a boy. I've played the one in control. I'm whoever I need to be to get the job done. And my boss has sent me into some pretty serious shit. The takeaway is that the Greek knows you, and he chose well. I needed the connection to stay close."

Michael leaned back on the wall and ran his hand down his neck to soothe the pain. "What happens now?"

"My boss gets his high-priced lawyer to get me released once the threat to you is settled. The mess by the stairs will cause a ruckus tonight, but no one else was in that stairwell. If we're lucky, they'll think the two went at each other. We just sit tight and wait. You stay here. Stay here so no one gets a look at that neck."

"I owe Bruce two joints. He'll be coming around in another hour."

"Give them to me and tell me where I can find him."

"Search out Sam in the laundry. He'll bring you to him. You're collecting as well. Tuck it in your waist or in your shoe. They won't search you this time of day." Michael got up slowly from his bunk and lifted the mattress for access to his contraband. "Was that really your mother that visited?"

"Well, yeah. She misses me," Roy said.

Michael nodded and handed over the weed. "I don't expect you'd want to continue what we had going."

"Don't see why not."

Michael smiled and rubbed again at his neck. "Because when I saw you at those two, I swear, I think I fell in love."

Roy shook his head. He pulled his shirt up and tucked the joints in the waistband of his pants. "The Viking gets back, you tell him you feel sick, you might be contagious. Turn over and get some rest."

≈

Galen Stathakis entered his office. He pulled the pack of cigarettes from his shirt pocket and sat at his desk. Jimmy Tens sat back on the couch and straightened his pant leg as Galen lit up.

"The exchange is in two days. We'll have her back in two days," Jimmy said.

"You made contact with this guy?"

"He phoned Byrd."

"Why two days?"

"He's being pulled back to Washington. He wants an exchange and then be gone. I don't like the wait any more than you. I can't see any way around it."

Galen took a slow, long drag on his cigarette and tapped off the ashes into the ashtray. "We need to plan. Where's the meet?"

Jimmy sat forward. He leaned his forearms on his thighs, clasping his hands together. "We won't know until day of. Byrd told me I'm to steer clear of the guy until then. Byrd's going to swing by here during his shift tonight. When he can break free."

"Why don't you head upstairs and get some sleep? I'll be up when the man shows."

"Another thing, Galen. Michael Ranney. If he's going to be hit, it'll be now. We might want to get a couple guys on him."

"He's got protection." Galen knew the Billerica House of Correction held inmates serving short sentences. But he also knew the jail kept men awaiting trial and men transitioning out of higher-security prisons like Walpole and Concord. It would be in those fluid stays that Galen saw potential for trouble for Michael, and he took precautions accordingly.

Jimmy stood and made his way out the back up to the apartment.

Galen stood from the chair with effort. The years were beginning to take a toll on his joints. He walked out to the bar and motioned to Tao for a drink. He extinguished his cigarette in an ashtray.

Tao set Galen up with an ouzo. "What's the word?"

"We'll have her in two days."

The two kept their voices low, keeping the others farther down the bar in the dark.

Tao stepped back a step and set the bottle on the shelf without turning his head. "That's a long time."

"Unavoidable. Officer White is stopping in so we can work this through." Galen glanced down the bar at Brendan McHugh. The Irishman tended to imbibe in step with the mood of the people around him. And with the tension, secrecy, and somber goings-on of late, his drinking had tapered off. "You doing all right, Brendan?" Galen called down.

"Too depressing around here to have a good time," Brendan said. He moved his glass around in a small circle on the bar.

Sally James sat in front of the taps. Her attention was out one of the small windows beside the door. The wind was causing tree limbs and electrical lines to sway.

Galen drank the ouzo and pushed the small glass forward. "Sally. Would you jump behind the bar for a bit? I need to send Tao out."

"I can do it," Brendan said.

Galen shook his head as Sally stood from her stool. In seconds, she tied a loose bun at the back of her head. She left two loose strands of hair out to hang and frame her face. She walked past Tao behind the bar. Her blouse was long-sleeved and covered her collarbone, but it had a scooped back and showed her smooth skin and the line of spine traveling up her long neck.

Galen gave Tao a small smile. "Head over to my place. Back corner of the woodshed. The kid from Boston dropped off Jimmy's piece, and I tucked it there until Jimmy could swing by the house. He's sacked out upstairs, and I want him to get as much downtime as possible."

≈

The weather was picking up in severity. Tao made his way through downtown in his truck as the sky darkened considerably. Up ahead on the sidewalk he noticed the form of a familiar figure. The hunched-over man was dressed in a long, tan trench coat, rumpled, like the one Columbo did his detecting in. He had a choppy gait and held down his hat as the wind tugged at it. Tao had never seen Jacob Collier outside of his home before. He was an odd sight walking the empty sidewalk, determined to battle with the forces of nature.

Tao pulled over his truck. He leaned over and cranked down the passenger window. "Jacob. What you doing, man? You need a lift?"

Jacob looked over and squinted at Tao. A sign of recognition came over his face, and he took the chance of losing his hat as he reached out with both his hands to open the truck door. Jacob struggled to pull himself up and into the vehicle. He reached for the grab handle to steady himself and slide onto the seat. Tao looked over as he put the truck into drive. He thought of Jayne. Of the first few times she rode with him and the effort it took for her to seat herself. It was comical at the time. Now he felt a dead weight, like a rock, in his stomach.

"What's got you out in this weather, Jacob? Where're you headed?" Tao asked.

Jacob cleared his throat as if preparing to talk after having no occasion to speak for a few days. "Over by Donahoe Park."

"What's over there?"

"My son."

"You have a son? I didn't realize that. How old is he?"

"Twenty-six."

"How come I never knew you had a son?"

Jacob stuffed his hands in his coat pockets. He pulled the long garment tighter around his body. "He's never been with me. His mother chose to raise him herself. He's gotten into trouble last few years. She told me the boy was wrapped up in drugs and stealing from her. So she worked to get him into a program to get straight. Last I spoke to her, she said she wasn't as worried about him anymore. He was straightening himself out. She was looking forward to getting back down to Florida."

"You couldn't make things work between you two."

"His mother and me? We were never together-together."

As Tao drove the truck to a quieter part of the city, rain began to fall in sheets. The sound of it beating on the hood and the top of the truck, and noise of the wipers, filled the cab. Tao cranked down his window an inch. He needed the air to clear the windshield, which had begun to fog over. He slowed and leaned forward over the steering wheel to squint ahead.

"It's getting bad out here," he said. "You didn't say why you're out walking in this weather. You could have picked a better night to go visiting."

"My son called me. He's never called me before. He asked to stay with me a few days. Said he was on his way over, but he never showed. He's never asked anything of me before. It's got me worried."

Tao nodded. He leaned back as the window cleared. He drove

through a neighborhood leading up to the park and eventually swung a right. He slowed the truck to a crawl, and Jacob pointed to a large house completely in the dark. A green Nova was parked in the driveway. Tao and Jacob got out of the truck and walked briskly up the narrow pebble path to the house. They climbed the front steps. Tao pulled open the storm door and knocked. He rose on his toes and peered in the small circular window on the door. But with the interior dark, he saw nothing. Jacob pulled himself closer to Tao, under the eaves, as rain pelted the two of them.

"No one's home, Jacob."

"Can we wait a bit longer? Or get inside? My son wouldn't have called me unless he was in trouble. He never called me before. Even for money."

"All right. But not here. You go around back. I'll grab a flashlight and meet you at the back door." Tao sprinted off the steps to get to his truck. He opened the door and pulled the seat forward. He found his flashlight in his white tool bucket. He ran to the back of the house with his shoulders hunched. The rain had turned the dirt to mud at his feet. The tired, weath-er-beaten back steps vibrated as he ran up and met Jacob at the door.

Tao turned the flashlight first to the knob and then through the window above. He knocked and scanned the beam across the kitchen. He reversed its direction on seeing what appeared to be the figure of a man sitting in a chair at the kitchen table. Tao knocked again. He held out his right arm. "Stand back a minute, Jacob."

Tao turned the flashlight around in his hand. He broke out one of the four panes of glass on the door. He cleaned off the shards and tenta-tively reached his left hand in. He pulled his body up closer to the door and reached down to the knob on the inside. The door opened. Tao stepped in with his eyes trained on the dark figure at the table. He felt around with the palm of his hand on the wall. He flipped up a switch, silently praying his instinct would fail him as Jacob pushed at his back to join him in the room.

There in the chair sat John "John Doe" Donato, eyes and mouth open, head back and arms hanging limp at his sides. Limbs that provided the balance he needed in death. In the center of his forehead was a bullet hole, a fatal wound accounting for the mess of blood down the back of his chair and in a pool on the floor.

"Jesus, I'm sorry, man," Tao said without turning his head to Jacob. He stepped to the phone that hung on the wall at the end of the cabinets. It had a long spiral cord that reached the floor. He lifted the receiver and found no dial tone. Tao hung it up and turned to see Jacob pull out a chair and take a seat at the table.

A banging sound came from the floor above. Tao looked at the ceiling and listened to a muffled, feminine cry for help. He rushed down the hall and bounded up the stairs, two at a time. He saw the boards nailed across the door as he neared the top of the stairs. He trained his flashlight more directly on them. Another cry came from within, and Tao recognized the voice.

His eyes widened in wonder. "Jayne? Jayne, that you?"

"Turn on the light. Please. I can't. It's too dark."

Tao stepped onto the landing and flipped the switch on the wall. He could see the light shine out from around the seams of the door. The sound of Jayne sliding her body slowly down the door to sit on the floor was unmistakable.

"Jayne. I need to get a crowbar to get these boards off. You're safe now."

"Don't leave me."

"The light stays on, Jayne. I'll be two minutes. I'm not going anywhere without you." Tao turned and ran down the stairs. He flew through the kitchen and out to his truck. He grabbed up a claw hammer, a crowbar from under the seat, and a mallet from the white tool bucket. He ran back through the rain that had not let up and bounded back up the stairs.

Jacob still sat staring at a set of glass salt and pepper shakers in the center of the table.

Tao reached the hallway and switched on the light with an elbow. He turned his head back to the table. "Jacob. Run next door and call for help."

Jacob rose as instructed and reached for the door. Tao made his way up to the bathroom door, setting the tools on the hallway floor. He pried up the edge of each board, two across and one as an anchor, so he could find leverage with the crowbar. In moments, he had the boards off and opened the door.

Jayne stood with a hip leaning on the sink. Her hair was down. Her pants were tied in a knot at the waist, their legs rolled up to her ankles. And she wore a sweater that hung loose on one side and reached nearly to her knees.

Jayne tucked her hair back, behind her ear, and out of her eyes. "How did you find me?"

"Not now. Let's get you out of here."

Tao followed Jayne down the stairs after abandoning his tools. He placed his palm on her lower back when they reached the first floor. They walked down the hallway to the kitchen and heard the back door open.

Tao placed his hand up on her shoulder. "There's a body in the kitchen, Jayne. If you need to, shut your eyes and I'll get you out the door."

Jayne stepped forward and entered the room. She took in the scene. John Doe remained in his seat at the table. Jacob Collier sat to his right. Jayne walked over and grasped one of Jacob's hands and squeezed, not knowing why Jacob was there, away from the safety of his home. But she instantly noticed a sadness etched on Jacob's face as he looked over at the dead man.

"Jayne. Let's get down to the truck," Tao said. He opened the door and looked down at her feet. They were clad in the heavy wool socks. He stepped over and lifted her up in his arms, bracing her from under her knees and around her back near her shoulder blades. She appeared even tinier than days before, more fragile.

Jayne reached down and tugged on the arm of Jacob's coat.

"I'm going to stay here awhile and sit with John," Jacob said. He looked up at Jayne and gave her a weak smile.

Tao maneuvered Jayne out the door. He carried her down the back steps. He headed toward his truck, and one of his feet slipped a moment in the mud as he turned. A loud shot rang out from the trees, over the sound of the driving wind and rain. Tao fell to his knees and eased Jayne to the ground. "Run," he said.

Jayne set her palms on the earth and slid over as Tao laid his body back flat. He held a hand over a wound above his collarbone. She added her hand on top of his to help stem the flow of blood. She breathed in deep, and tears welled in her eyes.

Jayne was pulled briskly to her feet. Thomas Curry held firmly to her arm and pulled her to his side. His other hand held a gun directed down at Tao's chest.

"Don't shoot him. I'll go with you, if you just—don't shoot him," Jayne said.

Tao shut his eyes and dropped back his head to the ground in defeat. Curry pulled Jayne back roughly toward the trees and in the direction of the cemetery. They traveled back over their ingress. It was the same familiar path of branches and stones, but with a harder rain that soaked the soil and turned the pine leaves on the ground slick.

Within feet of the stone wall, Jayne dropped down, using a tactic Jimmy Tens showed her to break out of a hold. She dropped like a dead weight, but Curry never let go. He was a worthier opponent and appeared ready for the move. He gripped Jayne's arm like a vise. But as he leaned down to get momentum to pull her up, he overcompensated a hair. And it was all she needed.

Jayne had a second to brace her knee on the ground. With quick reflexes, she reached around with her right hand under the sweater. To the back pocket of the pants, where she had tucked her blade before nestling in the bathtub with the blanket and pillow that John provided for the long, long wait in the dark.

As Curry pulled her up, she was at the perfect height and angle. She didn't stab. She slashed—deep, upper thigh, near Curry's groin. It brought him to the ground, and he released Jayne's arm to hold both hands over the wound, two fingers still wrapped around the butt of the gun. Jayne jumped up and ran back through the woods, stepping here and there on one of the pant legs that had unraveled. She ran awkwardly but determinedly until she reached Tao, who still lay on his back, looking up to the sky in the unrelenting rain. Jayne skidded to her knees and placed her hands over his wound as sirens were heard on the street. Lights of police and emergency vehicles lit up surrounding homes, the green Nova, and Tao's truck.

"Tell them everything, Jayne," Tao said.

"I don't know anything."

Tao covered her hands with one of his own. He relaxed back and let darkness engulf him as he began to drop into unconsciousness.

Jayne's tears were washed clear by the rain, and she looked back, over to the steps, to the light of the kitchen. Light that illuminated a man who sat and kept company with the remnants of his departed son's soul.

≈

FBI Agent Thomas Archibald Curry willed himself to stand. He had chosen not to shoot the girl, and he was curious if he was slipping or if he merely accepted the fact that he was irrevocably compromised. After setting his gun in its holder under his arm, he made his way to the wall while dragging his leg. He pulled his necktie down at his collar and used both hands to untie it. First a climb over the wall, then he would tie the leg and make his way over to his car. He sat on the wall and swung his good leg over. He grabbed his other pant leg and lifted.

Curry emitted a groan. It was low and sustained because he felt something give, and the lightheadedness he experienced gave him an answer to his question. The nick the girl had put on his femoral artery was now a tear.

He felt the blood flow. Already saturated with water, he felt the warmth as it coursed down his leg. He had a general knowledge of anatomy, and he knew he was marked for death. He walked only a few rows before reaching out to a stone for balance. He settled himself down with his back to the base of a grave marker that gave the remains below its name and recorded time among the living. He looked up and into the soulful eyes of the Ayer Lion, a white marble sculpture close enough in size to appear real in Curry's mind. The lion had a large mane and was a beast at regal rest who looked down with an expression Curry beheld as all-knowing. The animal sitting in his final judgment.

≈

The sixties had been about seeing and reading the signs. These early years of the new decade had the whiff of decay and a fraying of the moral fabric of society as it unfurled. A strong reckoning of conscience was reachable, but at a distance, on the horizon.

Thomas Curry played his part in reaching that horizon by expiring on the plot of soil on which he fell. The rains lessened to showers and his brethren arrived, not to mourn over the coming days but to attempt to unravel the damage one man had wielded. His corpse, lying in repose, was lit artificially until dawn. His form was thrust into the light with no voice to object. Silenced by a girl of sixteen.

CHAPTER TWENTY-SIX

Tao awoke to a tickling sensation on his right sole. He opened his eyes and looked down to the foot of the bed he lay in. Jimmy Tens stood with Tao's foot in his hand, running the point of a pen from heel to toe.

"What are you doing?" Tao said.

"Checking for the Babinski reflex. And to wake you—with success, I might add."

"Knock it off."

"We need to talk. Before your folks arrive." Jimmy covered Tao's feet with the blanket.

Tao nodded.

"The FBI are down on the first floor talking with Jayne. That gives us only a short window," Jimmy said.

"They let you in here?"

"Byrd relieved the local boy in blue on your door."

"So that's why I rated a private room."

Jimmy shrugged. "Do you remember what happened on Deerfield Street?"

"I got shot. Jacob's son is dead. And the fed grabbed Jayne." Tao tilted his head before continuing. "She made her way over to me before the cavalry arrived, though. How'd she break free?"

"You're to be proud of our Jayne. Used her knife to send the G-man down to Hades."

Tao took a deep breath and closed his eyes. "How is she?"

"Good. She snapped at one of the agents who put his hand on her arm downstairs. She's got nothing to give them other than being grabbed off the street by some maniac."

Tao opened his eyes. "Keep it that way. At least until the heat dissipates. And while we're at it—give me a rundown of what Galen wants me to tell these goons."

"You picked up Jacob on the road to his son's house. Gave him a lift. Jacob only knows what transpired on Deerfield Street. And speaking of Jacob, Jayne tells me the crazy loon's got buried treasure in his yard. Cash in the ground. His kid tucked it there for safekeeping. Figure I'll give him a short time to settle back in then offer him a hand taking stock."

Tao pushed his arms on the rails to sit up farther on the bed but halted and winced as pain spiked through his upper body. "So, you think they're not going to probe further after I stumbled on Jayne, who's been living with me from before her mother died. How do I explain that I never reported the girl missing if she was holed up there in the house?"

"She's a teenager. You thought she was rebelling after the death of her mother. Thought she was crashing at a friend's house."

"You want me to explain it as a coincidence?"

"Why not?"

Tao cracked a smile. "What is that? The 'small world' ploy?"

"Look. These government guys are trying to get out of town with the least bit of egg on their faces. They have enough troubles as it is, if you follow the papers. With Jayne, it's an obvious case of self-defense. She was abducted, kidnapped, and held by a man in their employ. Do you know how many psychological tests they run these guys through? They'd never live down the press on this horror show. And they've got John Doe's death to deal with."

Tao adjusted the pillow under his head. "Do you think they know what's been going on with their guy?"

"Bet they went balls to the wall on him as he drew his last breath. Found his bank accounts, his connections. It's what these guys do. Any location, any person he came in contact with. The whole organization mines for information. If they haven't found the trail of his criminal activities by now, this country is in deep shit."

"And the other players?"

"Who?" Jimmy asked.

"Michael Ranney, Margaret Ranney, Ray Hamel."

"We're not offering up anything. None of it need come to light."

Tao motioned to the water jug on a tray beside the bed. Jimmy poured him a cup and steered a straw to Tao's mouth.

Tao took a good, hearty drink and rested his head back on the pillow. "They won't press on how Jayne is wrapped up in this? Why she was taken in the first place?"

"I'm telling you. They want out of this town. They want to take their man's remains and ship them to his family for proper burial. How they chalk up how he came to be deceased is on them. Let them think he had a few screws loose. Toting around a basket of sexual perversions. Anything so they get on their way and we can get back to our lives. It's already been suggested that if you and Jayne promise to keep quiet about the actions of their agent, they won't seek charges or put either of you through hoops. They'll have you sign some super-secret FBI confidentiality agreement to make sure none of this comes back on their people. Then they'll be on their way."

A whistle came from the door, and Byrd poked in his head. "My guy's due back any minute. You guys good?"

Jimmy nodded. The door closed, and Jimmy set the water back on the table. "When they're done with you, call the nurse and get yourself out of here. It's not the surgery that kills you, it's the infections you catch after. Hospitals are a breeding ground. Call the bar, and we'll swing by and meet you at the door. Any aftercare you need, I can handle. Man, you got lucky with where that bullet hit. I thought the FBI were expert marksmen."

"I slipped in the mud." Tao set his elbow on the bed and held up his hand.

Jimmy clasped it.

"You'll check on Jayne?" Tao asked.

"Last I saw, Galen stood with his back to the door of the room they have her in, a scowl on his face and cursing in Greek. He'll stand there strong until they release her." Jimmy walked to the door and turned. "Be careful when they question you. They're good with mind games. If you don't want to answer, tell them you're in pain and want to rest."

"Not a stretch."

Jimmy stepped out of the room, and the door closed slowly at his back. Byrd stood from the chair at the door and motioned with his chin to the officer walking their way from down the corridor. The man was returning to his post.

And from the opposite direction, Veronica Nowak walked up the hallway with a metal-backed chart in her hand and a French twist in her hair. She passed by the two and gave a wink and demure smile to Jimmy. He followed her with his eyes as she walked by, returning the smile. He turned his head to Byrd as Byrd took notice of Jimmy's appearance, head to foot. The ripped jeans, the paint-spattered boots with loose laces, the torn and worn jacket. Byrd glanced down at his own uniform, from his regulation shoes, up and over his blues. He ran two fingers down one side of the collar of his shirt, down to the point.

"I don't get it," Byrd said.

Jimmy laughed. "Maybe she's not one of those gals to take to the uniform. Likes her men rough-and-tumble."

≈

Michael Ranney was led into the visitors' room of the Billerica House of Correction with six other inmates. The bulk of the men with visitors were already assembled in the room. Jayne sat at a table facing him. She sat forward and leaned her elbows on the table, arms crossed, waiting.

Michael frowned on seeing a scar marring her hairline above her temple. It looked too new to be left over from Margaret. "Hi, kid. They found you all right?"

"Great observation."

"What're you doing here?"

"To mess with you. Why else would I schlep my way here?"

"Who drove?"

"Jimmy. He's out waiting in Galen's Caddy. You going to sit or what?"

Michael sighed as he sat down. "I had a pretty close call recently. Why don't you ease up on me a little?"

Jayne picked at her sleeve with her thumb and first finger. "Galen gave me the honor of giving you good news. And before you start with the questions, let me get this all out."

"Spill."

Jayne leaned in but kept her voice at the same volume so as not to attract attention. "You're safe. I'm safe and you're safe. And it's a minute too late for Mom, but the fed is dead."

"I haven't heard you call her Mom in years."

"She's gone now. Guess it's the time to appreciate the fact that she gave us life."

"Tried to beat it out of us, but you're right. We owe her that much."

"I don't want you worrying about me. I know what you did. Asking Galen to look after me. I don't need you to do that anymore."

"Is that right?"

"Tao gave me a place to crash. And Galen's going to keep me on. Let me work again as soon as he chills out. I'll know he's all right when he stops muttering to himself, smoking like a chimney. He's been hanging out at the Greek coffee shop by DeMoulas. He spends most of his days there. Since the cops got through with me, that is. Tao and Jimmy have been handling the action."

"I wish I could help. But I got at least another nine months in here."

"Not to be harsh, Michael, but it doesn't make much difference to me. I learned a long time ago not to count on you, and it frees me up not to wonder. I'm left with no expectations."

Michael coughed into his closed fist.

Jayne reached back for her braid and pulled it forward. She pulled at the strands of hair at the end of the tie. "I'd like time to get to know you better. Sit in back of the alley when Jimmy's grilling burgers. Hang out. But truth is, we've never had that. I forgive you for whatever guilt you carry. I've learned that I'm happiest when I'm figuring things out for myself."

"For a small kid, you sure know how to gut a guy." Michael ran a hand through his hair from his forehead back. "I'm thinking of skating to New York City after my stretch anyway. Got somebody who's invited me down. Thought I might see where it takes me." He shrugged once and slumped in dejection. "But—there's a very good chance he's shining me on."

"I don't get it."

Michael clarified the statement, more to himself than to his sister who sat across the table, engulfed in his old denim jacket. "It's what I would do."

≈

Brendan McHugh arrived at the Skillet with a bag of crullers and three cups of coffee set in a cardboard carrier. He set them down and pulled one of the cups out of the holder. He passed it over the bar to Sally James, who had stepped in to help Tao while he was on the mend.

Brendan read the question in Sally's expression. "You're pouring now, aren't you?" he said.

Sally smiled slightly and grabbed for a pint glass to fill at the taps. She had taken to wearing a leather cuff on her wrist similar to Tao's, but narrower, with the addition of a few colorful beads in a zigzag pattern. Tao eased behind Sally with a light hand to her hip. His right arm was in a sling to allow his collarbone to heal. It prevented him from moving in a way that would pull on his wound. He reached out his good arm and grabbed a bottle from the shelf. He filled the shot glass he had set in front of Brendan.

"How's the weather out there?" Tao asked.

Brendan finished his bourbon in one and reached for his pint as he settled on his stool. "As cold as a witch's tit."

Tao grabbed up a coffee and hooked the bag of donuts with the last two fingers of the same hand. He walked the bar, down to Jimmy Tens, and set down breakfast. With Galen over at the coffeehouse, the routine remained the same.

Jimmy was on the phone and scribbled a few notes on a small white pad. He suddenly looked up to the ceiling and sighed. "God save me." He hung up and reached for the coffee. "Dolt is calling back after an hour, telling me he changed his mind on a pick. They would never try that stunt with Galen. Do I look like an easy mark to you?"

Tao laughed as he turned and reached under the bar for the trash bin from the previous night. He stepped out from behind the bar and took the trash can down the back hall and out the door. To the left, in the alley, was Officer Byrd White in the driver's seat of his idling police cruiser.

Tao set down the can, and hunching his shoulders to the cold, he made his way over. He opened the passenger door and took a seat. "What you doing out here?"

"Thinking."

"And?"

"I have nightmares. Since starting the job, really. They're always about outcomes I can't control. But with this, I had my hand in. I think if I stepped back in the beginning. If I'd never visited Ranney or taken his call, it would have haunted me."

"What about Hamel? You good with turning a blind eye?"

"Ray got an official policeman's send-off with colors. More than he deserved in life. His daughter has a family she's raising and gossip or conjecture about her father will not help her in the neighborhood. Those neighborhoods are tight. Stories of twenty, thirty years ago are still being bandied about."

Tao adjusted the strap on his sling.

"How's your girl?" Byrd asked.

"She started back at school today. Talked about seeing to some 'cousins.' Not sure if I should be concerned or proud she's sounding all grown up." Tao looked over at Byrd and shook his head slightly. "She has a date on Saturday. Émile Savard—a Canuck. Can you run him and his family? See if anything pops?"

"Relax. It's just a date."

Tao nodded. "Don't know why I'm worrying—Jimmy's on point." He looked at the rear door of the bar and back at Byrd. "You on days now?"

"Switching shifts with a guy today. Someone put a word in, though. Recommending me for a job escorting the city manager. You don't think Galen knows anything about that?"

"Nah," Tao said.

"I'm going to pass. Going to work my way into plainclothes, but I'm going to do it on my own schedule."

Tao nodded and reached for the handle on the car door.

"You need to take Jayne Ranney off the street," Byrd said.

"Jayne's not some child we're exploiting, some innocent to the world. She's strong. And if you ask her, she'll say she's making the decisions now. And Galen, Jimmy, and I support her in any way she needs. It's a lot more than most have coming out of the gate."

"Fair enough."

"Anything else?"

"Let Galen know—now that his girl's back safe, we can both go back to what we do best. He'll have no hassles from me."

"Right on, man."

ACKNOWLEDGMENT

This book was a labor of love. One I could not have brought to completion without the help of others.

My deepest thanks to Carl McCarthy, Ryan Quinn, Allister Thompson, and Nuno Moreira of NM Design. David Shaughnessy for sharing his memories. The City of Lowell: a community that gifted me an extended family. Richard and Joan McCarthy for their early kind words and introduction to their generous son.

The Irish Writers Centre of Dublin for holding a Novel Fair and giving me the push of a deadline. Reedsy, New Hampshire Writers' Project, Grubb Street, Steven Lee Beeber, and The Lowell Sun for being a resource. The Pollard Memorial Library and other local libraries for offering me refuge. Jack Monaghan, Philip Stanway, and Claude Goulet for introducing me to Lowell. The friendship of Cathy Leary and Chris Alcorn of Furey's Café, along with Vasilios Βασίλειος Tzioumis and all those at Duffy's. James Sarantos and Robert McLaughlin, who dared in life to seize the days. Robert Joy, Brett Joy, David Grilli, and Luke Grilli for their support and gifting me a quiet workspace. Ryan Ackelsberg for his encouragement. My five siblings: Jack Monaghan, Ann Dosen, Tom Monaghan, Susan Monaghan, and Eileen Joyce for sharing the love of reading. My deepest gratitude to my beloved husband Trent and my family.

Made in the USA
Monee, IL
02 August 2020

37450281R00142